CHRISTMAS AWAKENING

AMISH CHRISTMAS BLESSINGS SERIES, BOOK 5

GRACE LEWIS

BOOK DESCRIPTION

In the season of giving, will Mary's longing to teach disrupt the Yuletide peace in her family?

In the quaint Amish town of Dalton in Kingston, the Yuletide season brings more than just snowflakes and sleigh bells for Mary and Moses Lapp. Amidst the twinkling Christmas lights and the scent of fresh pine, Mary Lapp, blessed with three beautiful children and a loving husband, finds herself grappling with a longing for something more. As the festive spirit envelops the town, her heart yearns to return to her passion for teaching, reigniting a spark that once brought her immense joy.

But as the snow blankets the peaceful streets, resistance comes from the most unexpected place

– her own home. Moses Lapp, her devoted husband, basks in the contentment of their thriving farm and the warmth of their family life. Unseen challenges begin to encroach upon his idyllic world. Clinging to faith and love, Moses is determined to face these trials head-on, yet he remains blind to the growing restlessness in his wife.

Their once harmonious home now echoes with the silent tension of unspoken dreams and unmet desires. Mary's resolve to teach clashes with Moses' wish for her to remain the heart of their home. As Christmas approaches, their disagreement casts a shadow over the festive preparations, and even their children sense the growing divide.

In this heartwarming tale set against the backdrop of an Amish Christmas, Mary and Moses must navigate the delicate balance between personal aspirations and familial responsibilities. Will the magic of the season guide them back to each other, or will their differences push them further apart? Can they find a way to blend Mary's dreams with the needs of their family, rekindling not just the spirit of Christmas but the flame of their love?

Unwrap the gift of love, understanding, and new beginnings in this captivating Amish romance, where the true meaning of Christmas shines through the struggles and joys of Mary and Moses Lapp.

～

The *Amish Christmas Blessings* series focuses on Mary and Moses Lapp's evolving relationship during the Christmas holiday season. In it, they learn the true meaning of family and belonging. Read this heartwarming holiday Amish romances knowing that you'll find uplifting stores of faith, forgiveness, hope and true to life angst that ends with a sweet happily-ever-after.

FOREWORD

This book is dedicated to you, the reader.

Thank you for taking a chance on me, and for joining me on this journey.

Do you want to keep up to date with all of my latest releases, and **start reading *Rumspringa's Promise, Secret Love* and *River Blessings*, exclusive spinoffs from the *Seasons of Love, Amish Hearts* and the *Amish Sisters* series, for free?**

Join my readers' group (copy and paste this link into your browser: *bit.ly/Grace-FreeBook*). Details can be found at the end of the book.

CHAPTER 1

Mary sat on her porch early in the morning, a shawl wrapped around her shoulders. It had snowed the night before, leaving the world white and perfectly ready for the coming Christmas season. It was not the snow that had her on the porch this morning. That honor went to her *kinner*: her eight-year-old twins, Faith and Elijah, and her beautiful young *dochder* Ruth who had come to their *familye* six years ago.

This was the first snow of the year, and it had come down gently. There couldn't have been more than a few inches of snow, which left plenty of space for her *kinner* to jump in the leaves that Moses had raked up yesterday.

Sitting on the porch with her, Addie held up a sample of crochet work. In the last few years, Mary had become rather good at crocheting. Despite her initial feelings about the craft, she had to admit that she liked it. She looked up when she heard loud giggles, louder than she would have expected from the *kinner* as they jumped around in the leaves.

She looked up to see the twins getting ready to throw their younger *schweschder* into the pile of leaves, which would have certainly scattered the leaves everywhere.

"You know," Mary said softly as she put her crochet sample in her lap to look up at the three of them, "if you make such a mess, you'll have to clean it up. And the snow has made it that much harder to clean up leaves today. Are you sure that you want to make a mess of these leaves?"

The three *kinner* looked at each other, then at Mary, and then all shook their heads.

"That's what I thought. Perhaps it's time for you three to come inside and get warm again before you continue," she said.

The *kinner* frowned.

"But *Mamm!*" Faith whined. "We're having fun."

"Then be careful you don't get too cold," Mary

said softly. "I don't want to see any of you get hurt either. Do you understand me?"

They all nodded.

With that, Mary returned her attention to the crochet work in her lap for but a moment.

The front door opened behind her, which meant that Moses was ready to leave for a day of work in his carpentry shop. That carpentry shop had been the reason that they had been able to afford what they needed, and she appreciated all the work that went into what he did. It was hard, strenuous labor, and he did it without a care in the world.

"I'll see you when I get home," Moses said before pressing a soft kiss to Mary's forehead. "Oh… that's a beautiful piece of crochet, dear. I cannot believe how *gut* you've gotten. I marvel at it." He gave her a smile, which only caused her to blush a little bit.

"*Danke.* See you when you get home, Moses," Mary said with a smile.

Faith, Elijah, and Ruth each hugged him on his way out of the yard, which Mary found an endearing sight. They were all clinging to his waist, with his arms around them as best as he could get them. Eventually, he sent them back to the yard, and off Moses walked towards his carpentry shop. He'd taken to walking there in the mornings and home in the evenings when it snowed to save the horse the trouble and to avoid it slipping on the ice and snow that had already melted and refrozen.

The *kinner* returned to playing in the leaves and snow, which was fine by Mary. She didn't get to enjoy a lot of time with Addie since having the *kinner* and Addie had never much been one to yearn for that milestone in her life.

Once Moses was out of sight, she turned to Addie with a soft sigh.

"Would you believe that I miss going to work every morning and feeling useful?" she said, shaking her head, "I love my *kinner*, and I wouldn't trade them for anything in the world, but they're at that age where I could get a job out of the *haus* during the school year and they wouldn't know the difference. Especially Ruth now."

"Well, I know that I may not have the best advice," Addie cautioned. "I don't entirely understand that feeling – having worked my entire life and never married. However, if that's truly how you feel, why don't you apply for the new teaching position at the school? They only have Edna Troyer in the school now. Elise left for

Pennsylvania to marry that *mann* she met while you were pregnant with the twins and hasn't returned since. They're struggling to fill the spot."

Mary pursed her lips.

"I suppose that is an option," she said. "I'm not sure that I could return to teaching considering that there are usually only unmarried women in those positions. But if the position needs to be filled desperately, there's no harm in trying."

"Especially since that is what most people will remember you for," Addie piped up. "That's where you got your start when Moses courted you, and I think that there are plenty of people who are getting ready to leave the school who fondly remember the years you taught."

"I'll have to look into it and see what I can do," Mary said, her voice lighter than it had been when wishing Moses a happy day at the carpentry shop. "But for now, what do you think of this piece? Moses said it was beautiful when he left, but… I don't know what I think of it. I spent a lot of time getting the stitches to work properly, but it still appears to be lopsided."

Addie laughed a little.

"That's what it is supposed to look like, Mary," Addie said. "It's not the easiest thing in the world, but you're right, it's far too lopsided. People would be able to tell immediately that you're learning if you wanted to put it into a larger piece."

Mary sighed.

"I suppose there's really nothing I can do about that unless I practice more," she said. "I crochet when the *kinner* take naps, but that's really the only chance I have to do it nowadays. When they were younger, I could crochet all day long unless they were feeding, because they slept a lot."

"And now it feels like they have far too much energy?" Addie raised an eyebrow.

"*Nee*, but there have been days I've wondered if I ended up taking them into the city by accident – knowing that there was no way I could have done that accidentally," Mary admitted. "They remind me of how I used to act as a *kind*, and I'm so sorry for my parents now. I wonder if Moses has the same thoughts or if he's been able to escape that kind of thinking."

"He may not escape all of it, but that doesn't mean he doesn't agree," Addie said. "Have you talked to Moses about your wish to have a job again? To feel useful?"

Mary wasn't entirely surprised the conversation returned to the topic of her feeling useless at home with the *kinner* since Ruth was the only *kind* at home during the school year and that would be changing come the start of the new school year.

"He was the one who suggested I take up crocheting, actually," Mary admitted. "He saw how much I wanted to do something with my hands, and we both knew I didn't have time to garden when the twins were younger. So, one day he surprised me with some beginner patterns, some yarn, and a few crochet hooks, just because he could. Said he thought this would be helpful and I could learn to crochet for our *kinner*."

"So that's where they all got those quilts that they talk about so proudly," Addie mused. "We've all wondered how they could have crocheted pieces of the quilts, too. You did that when they were young, didn't you?"

"I did. It was something that I could do while they were asleep without worrying too much about waking them up," she said, shrugging. "That was always the largest worry: waking them up when I was doing something while they slept. And I couldn't exactly leave the *haus* in case they woke up unless I wanted to have a sleeping *boppli* or two with me."

"Well, I know one thing from all the time

we've talked between when you first arrived in Dalton and now," Addie started, "and that is that you'll find something to keep you occupied. You always do."

Mary smiled.

"Well, for now, that's talking about crochet with you while we watch the *kinner* in the snow so that they don't make an utter mess of the yard, specifically that pile of leaves they've been jumping into all morning. I'm surprised no one has complained about hitting a stick yet with their knee, or their face. I don't want that to happen, but it's a leaf pile."

Addie nodded with a soft chuckle.

"Well, whatever the outcome of this morning's playtime is," she said, "I know that you'll be there to comfort them if something *does* go wrong. You've always been a *Wunderbar mamm*, Mary. I'm sure that you'll find something that will allow you to work and still take care of the *familye*."

Mary smiled at her friend.

"I think I needed to hear that from you. *Danke*," Mary said. "Now… what about your crochet? What have you been doing lately?"

Addie smiled and produced her crochet sample. It was made in white yarn, which she thought was rather adventurous. Usually, they attempted to crochet pieces that would match, color-wise, with the rest of their wardrobes.

"I've taken up some bridal crochet on the side," she admitted. "*English* brides will pay very well for crocheted flowers for their bouquets. I'm working on a calla lily right now. A white one, of course, and then some blue ones for the rest of the wedding party. At least, that's what the customer said. I have a lot of free time when no one's staying in the boarding *haus*. I don't charge much, but they appreciate my honesty about timing. The wedding this one is for is about a year away."

"I remember always thinking I'd do fake flowers at my wedding, before marrying Moses, anyway," Mary said. "Crocheted flowers would be such a beautiful keepsake for the wedding party, too, since they can be displayed like regular silk flowers without much worry about the fabric crinkling."

Addie smiled.

"I decided I'd do the bride's bouquet first because I love white calla lilies," she said. "The blue ones she wants are a little odd, but I suppose it makes sense if that's going to be the color scheme she wants. Then again, that's probably why she wanted fake flowers in the first place."

Mary nodded.

They finished their conversation a moment later because Ruth came running up to the porch crying about having fallen on a branch, exactly as Mary predicted someone might a few minutes ago.

"Well, I do believe that is my cue to go for the day," Addie joked. "I'll see you around, Mary. Will you be all right?"

"*Jah*. I can handle this," Mary said. "*Danke* for listening."

With that, Addie gave the *kinner* hugs and made her way back to the lodging *haus*. As Addie disappeared into the distance, Mary took the *kinner* inside to warm up by the fireplace and to treat Ruth's injured knee.

Though she loved all three of them, Mary couldn't exactly lie to herself and say she was not thrilled about the idea of applying for the teaching position. Addie knew her far too well.

CHAPTER 2

Moses had only been at his shop for a couple of hours before trouble set in. He'd been doing this for many years, and he knew his business well. He also knew the best places to get wood in the surrounding wooded areas to avoid problems such as termites and ticks being transferred into his customers' homes via his products.

He and his *daed* had both prided themselves on the quality of their furniture. Their reputations preceded them in the community, and in the last few years, Moses had decided to expand his business to supply the nearby *Englisch* city as well. There were plenty of *Englischers* who had heard of the good quality Amish materials that were built here, and so his business had grown.

And it was a good thing, too. For a while, he and Mary had had three *kinner* under the age of five. Now, they were getting into the school years and such, but it was still a hard thing to take care of all three of them on a tight budget. The decision to allow more *Englischers* to order from his shop had allowed him to commission some of the largest projects he'd ever worked on, from which he'd earned good money.

The only reason he cared was so that he could be sure he was giving his *familye* and his community a good future. As the elder of the community now that Joseph had passed away, he had to think about everyone and not just Mary and his *kinner*.

"Moses? Are you in?"

A voice caught his attention just as he was about to take his lunch break and enjoy the scenery for the first time after the freshly fallen snow because he'd been working so hard all morning. He had a commission due in a week, and he was rather close to finishing it. If he delivered it early, he had a feeling his client would be happy.

Moses walked into the front section of the store, where he had a few pieces on display for craftsmanship purposes and a window to allow people to see if he was at work.

"How may I help you? Are you here to place another order, Gerard?" Moses smiled a little.

Gerard Riverton – the man standing in front of him – had placed an order for a living room set. It consisted of a couch, a loveseat, two chairs, a coffee table, and two end tables. As well as an entertainment set, which Moses had never attempted before. It had been a large, ambitious project, and he had charged by the piece so that he could do each piece properly.

"That living room set you sold me is infested with termites!" Mr. Riverton's voice came at him as if he had tampered with his *familye's* safety on purpose. "I want a refund *and* damages. I've had a lawyer work up the numbers."

He presented Moses with a small piece of paper that showed the payments that had been made for each piece of furniture in the set, and what they were wanting to claim for damages. The final number was in the thousands.

Moses's heart sank. This would leave him utterly destitute, and it would leave his *family* in the worst place they had been since Moses married Mary.

"Mr. Riverton, please," Moses said softly, "I'm

sure we can come to some kind of compromise. Do you have the furniture still? I'd like to see it. Perhaps I can replace the damaged pieces before the termites do any more damage to the set."

"I've thrown them away to prevent my family from getting hurt. It's *Christmas time,* for goodness sake! How could I allow the termites to spread and ruin all of the preparations my wife has made for the holiday?" Mr. Riverton said sharply. "Your reputation preceded you as a place to get wooden furniture made with top quality wood. To get a whole set infested with termites is absolutely unacceptable! I will be back if you do not find a way to come up with this money, and you'll sincerely wish that you had."

Mr. Riverton turned on his heel and walked out of the shop in a huff. Moses was only thankful that the confrontation had taken place when no one else was in the store. He gulped hard once he was sure that Mr. Riverton had left without any intention of returning today.

The first thought Moses had was that he needed to finish lunch and then head into the city. There were a few carpenters who had stores just on the outskirts of the city who might be able to help him navigate an unhappy *Englisch* customer. He hoped they'd be able to do something for him, because he was entirely at a loss as to how to proceed with this. He'd offered to undertake any repairs for free, and he was worried this would absolutely bankrupt him and his *familye* if he didn't find a way to satisfy Mr. Riverton.

After eating the sandwich that Mary had made him for lunch, Moses closed up the shop for the day and returned home. His *familye* appeared to be out, but they had left the horse and buggy. That was perfect.

Moses hooked the horse up to the buggy and made the long trip out to the city. His first stop was the first carpenter shop he saw, whose owner he knew. They had all been trying to get to know each other to help avoid troublesome customers. Moses was often the last to get the information just because he lived so far away.

He walked in to find no customers on the floor. There appeared to be no signs of any presence in the shop, but he walked to the desk and rang the bell.

"Hold on!"

Jonathan Stanton's voice came from the back of the store, and Moses smiled. He had managed to find a good time to drop in.

"Ah, Moses. What brings you here today?"

"I appear to have an unsatisfied customer and

I was hoping to get your take on the situation," Moses admitted.

He frowned a little as he looked around the shop. It was odd, being here looking for help instead of looking to others in the community for help. However, he had a feeling that the only person who could help him with an irate *Englischer* customer was another *Englischer* who knew the drill.

"Well, what's the problem?" Jonathan put down the water bottle he was holding to focus his attention solely on Moses. "It's odd to see you here over something like this, and I'm concerned. Do you think it's going to ruin your shop if you can't find a way to get it taken care of?"

"More than my shop, Jonathan," Moses started. Then he shared the story of what had happened when the man came into the shop. "And I can't replace the pieces that have termites because he's thrown the furniture away already. What am I to do? That kind of damage and compensation will leave me and my *familye* destitute, Jonathan."

"Relax, Moses," Jonathan said softly. "Do you have insurance? That'll usually pay for damages like this, especially since you're usually pretty good about delivering termite-free work."

"I don't have insurance. We don't do that in the community." Moses pursed his lips. "What am I supposed to do without insurance? I don't have that kind of money, and I don't know that I could come up with it easily."

He held his hands up, attempting to calm him down.

"I don't know, but the rest of us are here if you need help," he said softly. "But for now, it's getting late, and you've probably got a long buggy ride home. Why don't you go home and try to relax for now? He's only just made the complaint, so you've got some time before he is going to threaten legal action if it's only about the money. I've had customers like that, but usually ,they have pictures. Ask to see if he took pictures next time you see him."

Moses nodded slowly. Amish customers would have brought the furniture back or asked him what to do about it, but an *Englischer* could take photos to bring in, especially if they lived quite a distance from Dalton.

"*Danke*," Moses said. "I think I just needed another point of view on the situation. I think I'll go home and have a good dinner with my *familye*."

"There you go," Jonathan said with a smile. "I'll see you later, then, if this doesn't resolve?"

Moses shrugged before heading out to his buggy.

Once there, it didn't take him long to make sure that he was going to be home in time for dinner. He loosened the reins from their hitching and made his way back toward Dalton.

Upon arriving home, Moses found Mary preparing dinner. How lucky she was not having to worry about any of the things he had to face: the wellbeing of the community, the financial prospects of their *familye*, and such like. Certainly, she didn't have to worry about one customer financially ruining them if due care was not taken.

He took in a deep breath and put on the bravest face he could for Mary. He didn't want to worry her any more than necessary, but he knew that he would switch places with her in a heartbeat had this not been a man's job.

The *kinner* practically tackled him with hugs when they saw him walk through the front door. He hardly had enough time to close the door before his arms were around the lot of them, holding them indoors as he slammed the door with his foot to make sure that no one escaped into the cold before dinner. Or worse, that dinner would go cold.

"*Daed!* We missed you," Faith said. "Where did you go that you were gone so long?" She looked up at him with sparkling eyes as if she was more excited to see him than she was about the snow on the ground that morning.

"I had a lot of work to do today, Faith," he replied softly. "It took me longer than I thought it would to finish it. And I had to make a couple of deliveries, so I had to take the buggy around."

"That would explain why it was gone when we returned from seeing some friends," Mary said as she walked into the room. "I'm glad to see you made it back safely, Moses. It looks like it's going to snow all night, too."

"I was worried about that on my ride," Moses said as the *kinner* pulled away from him.

He gave Mary a gentle hug, resisting the urge to hug her tight and tell her that everything would be all right. He didn't want to make her worry.

"Dinner smells great, Mary," he continued. "What are we having?"

"One of your favorite stews, Moses," she replied softly. "I thought it would be best on this snowy day."

Moses smiled at her with a nod. He wished he could muster the usual enthusiasm, but she appeared to understand that travel was more than just a part of his day today. She pulled away to set the table, asking Faith and Ruth to help. Moses played with Elijah before they all sat down to dinner.

CHAPTER 3

The next morning, Mary was already a little weary and exhausted from working with her *kinner*. They were loud, boisterous, and excited. Ruth was excited to see the school *haus* where she would be attending school starting this coming year The snow that had fallen during the night had only made it harder to get around. She made sure everyone bundled up, though Elijah absolutely hated the coat he was supposed to wear because it was woolen and itchy.

"Come on, Elijah," Mary said softly. "We have to leave if we're going to be on time."

He finally put his coat on after learning that they were going to be late if he didn't, but he made no bones about complaining about it. She

wondered if he was so grouchy this morning because he hadn't slept well, but there was hardly
time for getting to the bottom of what was going
on for the moment.

She could do that after she had gone to see
Edna Troyer about the job. Her friend was now a
senior teacher in the community, and there was
something *wunderbar* about that. Edna had been
one of the teachers when she had first arrived in
Dalton, and to see her grow to the point where
she could be considered a senior teacher was
great.

Thankfully, Faith, Elijah, and Ruth all behaved
on the way to the school *haus.* They were all too
excited about seeing the place to worry about
where they were going to make trouble. Mary
hoped that the walk to the building would help
them get some of their boisterous energy out of
their systems.

"Here we are," Mary announced as they came
to the school *haus.*

It hadn't changed much since she had first arrived in Dalton all those years ago. The roof had
been replaced shortly after she had arrived, and it
appeared to be in need of another repair, but that
was the only major damage she could see due to
the weather. Something always broke in the

winter with such heavy snowfalls, no matter how well they reinforced the roof.

Thankfully, it was always over Christmas when it could easily be fixed.

They walked in and found Edna Troyer in the room.

"I want the three of you to be on your best behavior," Mary said softly as they started towards Edna. "This is very important, and I know that you're excited to be here, but please... be *gut*."

They all gave her a nod.

Mary didn't know how long this was going to last. She hoped quietly that Edna didn't need to ask much of her since they had worked together years ago and she most likely remembered Mary's abilities as a teacher.

"I'm glad to see that you were able to *kumm* today, Mary," Edna said. "Please, take a seat. I know it's a little cold in here, but with the roof leaking, I decided not to light a fire because the leak would extinguish it before it could warm the room up much."

"Perhaps you should talk to Moses about getting the roof fixed," Mary suggested. "I'm sure that he would be happy to help."

"I have that on my list of things I need to do, I promise," Edna replied. "Though, I must say that it is a little odd to see a *mamm* looking to apply for the teaching job. You brought the three *kinner* with you?"

"I didn't have anyone to watch them on such late notice," Mary admitted. "But with Ruth starting school next year, I felt that there was no better time to start looking for something that would allow me to feel useful again."

Edna smiled a little. She appeared to understand exactly what was going through Mary's mind, though Edna had no children herself. And after Elise had gone out to Pennsylvania to live with her *mann*, it made sense that they were having trouble filling this position. Elise had made such a fuss about getting the position back after Mary quit teaching that people were a little hesitant to fill it now that she was in Pennsylvania. However, they had all been reassured multiple times that Elise was not returning to Dalton.

"I see. Well, then, let us begin our little interview, shall we?"

Mary nodded.

As she was about to start, Faith came over and tugged on Mary's sleeve.

"*Mamm*, why are you talking to Edna?" Faith asked curiously. "I thought you were going to crochet for the money you want."

"I'm just looking into all of the options, Faith," Mary said softly with a smile. "Can you go make sure Elijah and Ruth are not getting into trouble for me? This is really important."

Faith nodded and walked away, but not before casting a glance back at Mary. She hoped that this was not going to happen throughout the interview, but she had a feeling that she could only hope in vain. They had been loud and excited at home. The walk did not appear to help with expending any of that energy.

"You had a question for me, Edna?"

"*Jah*. Is it being useful or that you're going to be lonely that you're looking at this job? Both are good reasons, but I'm simply curious. You've always said you loved being at home with your *kinner*. What changed?"

"As I said earlier, I want to be useful when I'm able to be," Mary replied. "If all three of my *kinner* are in school, then there's only so much I can do while I'm at home that doesn't include sitting and twiddling my thumbs waiting for everyone to return home. I'd rather have dinner on the table a little later than be stuck struggling with feelings of uselessness."

"That's a fair thing to wish for," Edna said. "It's just odd to see a married woman wish to be a teacher, though I understand it's quite the norm in an *Englischer* school."

Mary nodded slowly. This was indeed quite odd, to see a married woman wishing to have the position of a teacher in Dalton. But she didn't know what else to do. There was nothing else that would satisfy her need to get out of the *haus* and get a job quite like teaching would. She'd done all the teaching from home that she could at this age in the Amish faith that wasn't faith re-lated. She worried that if she continued to try to teach a religion her *kinner* which she had not held while growing up, she wouldn't know what to do when the day came to see them off into the *En-glischer* cities on *rumspringa* to see what they wanted to do with the rest of their lives. It had been partially a fluke that brought her to Dalton, but now that she was here, she didn't want to give it up.

"I just think I need to get out of the *haus* when the *kinner* are away at school, and this felt like the best option. I'll be home when they are, and I would not miss a day of their education. There's always going to be part of me that wants to teach. I am not the one to teach them religion, and that's all I'm doing at home with Faith and Elijah now. Very fulfilling," Mary admitted. "I love the faith, and my *kinner*, but there are just days when I don't know how else I'm going to handle it all."

Edna nodded.

"It's all very good information to have," she said softly. "But why teaching? Specifically? There are plenty of other things you could do if you want to feel useful and helpful around Dalton without having to teach."

"I trained to be a teacher before I came to Dalton, and it was being a teacher in Dalton that gave me the courage to find the life I wanted to live," Mary admitted. "I was miserable in Chicago because all I did was go to work and come home, and I had one friend. She didn't even really want to be friends through the nitty-gritty details of making such a big change, and I've hardly heard back from her since I was baptized. But I know the warning signs now, and I'm seeing the same thing starting to happen now that I'm home all day with the *kinner*, knowing that Ruth is going to be old enough to leave the *haus* for some time next school year."

"And you don't plan on changing your life as drastically now that you have a *familye*?"

"That's right," Mary replied. "Moses says I should find something that would keep me at home in case someone needs to stay home sick, but I'm sure that there are plenty of ways we could work around that if we needed to."

"Are you sure that you're going to be able to focus on the job when your plate is already full?" Edna raised an eyebrow. "You may be having a good conversation with me, but your eyes are tracking your *kinner* behind me because you want to be sure they're not getting into trouble. There's not much they could do here to get into trouble, Mary. That may not entirely be true at your home, but there's really nothing here that they could hurt themselves with. By design."

"I'm sure that I will be able to focus on the job," Mary said confidently.

Edna's next sentence was cut off by a crash behind them. Mary turned around as quickly as she could, getting up from the chair.

Elijah had been climbing on one of the bookshelves, and he was now under a pile of books with the shelf beside him. Faith stood beside him, her arms outstretched and her eyes wide with panic. It appeared that the two girls had managed to shove the bookcase to the side to keep their *bruder* safe, which at least made Mary feel better about not being able to keep an eye on them.

"I'll help you set the shelf back up."

"It's all right, Mary," Edna said softly. "I can do

it. Maybe you ought to take your *kinner* home. It seems that they're too excited to be unsupervised right now."

"Of course. I'm sorry about the bookcase," Mary said.

She gathered her *kinner* and walked out of the school *haus* with heated cheeks. Probably a flush of embarrassment. How could they have been doing something so reckless when she had asked them to be careful and make sure that they were behaving properly? They had been doing all right until Elijah climbed the bookcase and upended it.

Perhaps they hadn't had enough time to play today.

She kept an eye on them as they walked home together, although she could not help but feel disappointed. She was positive she wouldn't get the job now, not after Edna had seen her *sohn* do something like that in her school *haus*. She knew that they didn't behave like that for Edna while school was in session, for which she was thankful, but to do it during an interview. Did they not realize how serious it was?

Mary took in a deep breath and resolved that she was going to use this moment to teach them why she had wanted them to behave instead of getting angry at them. Anger would do nothing and fix nothing. Helping them understand why she had wanted them to be careful would be the better option.

When they arrived home, she had them all sit in the living room while she got a fire started. Then she shared her worries about what might have happened if that bookcase had landed on one of them.

CHAPTER 4

The next day, Moses returned to his shop only to find that the *Englischer* had decided that if he wasn't going to pay up immediately, he was going to be harassed until he paid. He now stood outside the store, yelling at other customers who were trying to make purchases. He warned them all how they shouldn't be supporting Moses because he was a crook.

It made him quite angry to hear someone accusing him of being a crook. However, there was little he could do about it right now. Instead, he just ignored the *Englischer*.

"What is Mr. Riverton doing outside?" Mr. Paul Troyer – Edna's *daed* – had come in to check on an order and frowned when he saw the *Englis-*

cher outside. "He's not doing you any favors by standing there calling you a crook. Is everything all right?"

"Everything's fine, Paul," Moses said softly. "He's just upset because something went wrong with his order. He only wants a refund and damages but he has disposed of the furniture we supplied, so I can't repair it." He shook his head. "Apparently, I'm a crook because I'd rather fix the furniture or have it returned than give him the refund without any reason to do so."

"That's not right," Paul said with a deep frown. "He's going to cost you business if he keeps this up. Is this the first time he's done it?"

Moses nodded.

"He came in yesterday to say that something had gone wrong."

"Well, then, he shouldn't be yelling that you're a crook. And you don't make as much money as he thinks you do from this. Have you told him that?"

"He didn't care," Moses admitted. "But it's not your problem, Paul. What have you come in for? Which order? I have a couple under your name."

Paul laughed a little.

"Right, right. I wanted to just check on the couch," he said. "It's getting harder to sit on my chairs and that's the one I'd rather have first, if you can make that happen."

"That order... let me go check on it, then," Moses said. "I have so many open orders right now that I've taken to tagging them all with paper on string to make sure I know whose is whose. I'll be right back."

"Take your time, Moses. I'm in no hurry."

With that, Moses walked into his carpentry workshop to check on the couch that he was going to deliver to Mr. Troyer. The only thing left to do was fashion the feet of the couch and fasten them on, then he could deliver it or have Mr. Troyer pick it up. That wouldn't take too long, but it would be long enough that he wasn't sure Mr. Troyer would want to wait in the shop until it was finished.

He returned to the front section of the shop to find Mr. Troyer looking around at the work he had on display.

"That couch only needs feet fashioned and added before it's ready to be delivered or picked up," Moses said. "I don't know that you'd want to wait while I fashion those in the shop or just wait until I come around with it."

"Think you can have it ready before Friday?"

"That should be doable," he said with a smile.

"Friday is when your other order should be done, as well, since it was smaller. A baby rattle. Do you have a *boppli* that you know of joining the *familye*?"

"It's actually for Edna to give to one of her friends who is expecting," Paul replied. "I hate to disappoint, but I don't think my *fraa* is having any more *kinner*."

"It's not her fault," Moses said. "Having *boppli* is an inexact science, and it's not always the trial we believe it is. I'll have those both done by Friday."

With that, Paul nodded with a smile.

As Paul left the shop, a local police car pulled up to the shop. Mr. Riverton stopped to talk to them, and then they came into the shop.

"Moses Lapp?" One of the officers looked over at him. "You the owner of this shop?"

"*Jah*," Moses said, hesitantly. "May I ask why you're coming here?"

"We've had multiple calls from the locals here in Dalton about someone harassing your shop and Mr. Riverton there says you're refusing to return his money," the officer said. "We can't do anything about him setting up shop on the sidewalk, but if he gets violent or decides to do it in the shop, you let us know."

"You can't... he's driving my customers away, Officer," Moses said as calmly as possible.

"We are aware of that, but there is no reason for us to intervene yet because he is on public property and, from what he has said, there is no case here for slandering."

Moses let out a sigh.

"All right. *Danke* for at least coming to see what was going on after the calls," he said. "I assume you're going to leave a number to call if I need it?"

They left him a business card, and he tucked it into one of the pockets on his apron. Then, to avoid getting himself any angrier, he started to work to calm himself. Carpentry had always helped him to recenter, but after hearing that there was nothing that the local police would do about this, it took more than just finishing a couch and baby rattle to make him feel all right.

He started on the next order in his queue as he tried to calm down.

How was he going to come up with the money to get Mr. Riverton to go away? And how could he prove that the furniture actually had termites if Mr. Riverton wouldn't speak to him except to tell him that he needed to come up with the money or he would regret it?

Moses took in a deep breath, letting it out slowly as he attempted to clear his head. There was only so much that he could do to make sure that there was money to pay out to this man. Perhaps Jonathan was right in that he needed to have insurance, but that wouldn't protect him right now. Not after someone had already lodged a complaint.

And, as far as Moses understood, insurance also required reasonable proof of the damages.

So, why was Mr. Riverton acting like he could get the money if he didn't prove any of the damages since he didn't have insurance? Was he simply taking advantage of the religious reasons that Moses had opted out of having insurance? Or was he trying to find a way of reimbursement for the money he had spent on that furniture – and more – because he was now going into debt for something else he needed?

He decided, as he was working on the next project, that he simply needed a way to come up with the money. As much as he thought that having Mary crochet some things and sell them would help, he knew that they wouldn't raise nearly enough money quickly enough. And Amish businesses prospered by word of mouth. That was how they got new clients.

Mary couldn't get a business up and running quickly enough to make any difference in getting the money to pay Mr. Riverton.

The last thing that he wanted to do to pay this man was to collect money from the community. That would perhaps shatter what trust they had in him as the youngest elder in the community's history. He didn't need to do that. Being the elder in the community was an honor, even though he wasn't nearly old enough to be considered an elder to those of the next generation.

He put down his tools as he thought, worried that he would mess up this order as he thought about how to come up with the money. Anger became part of the thoughts, and as much as he wanted to stop that from happening, he knew there was only so much that he could do to stop it. Though, perhaps anger was not the best word for what he was feeling.

Disappointment that he hadn't checked the wood as thoroughly as he thought he had. Fear that he would make his *familye* destitute, or worse, the community.

He decided to close up shop early and take a walk through the snow. As much as Moses didn't want to deal with this around Christmas time, he was afraid that he would have to do something before the holiday this year, or there would be no holiday to celebrate because of Mr. Riverton.

At least, to be able to celebrate with his *familye*.

As he walked through the snow, he listened to it crunch underneath his boots. It was not freshly fallen, and there had been some melting already. However, it was still crisp outside.

Icicles had gathered on the roof of his carpentry shop, and he stopped a moment and watched as the water started to trickle off the icicles as the sun hit them. Making deliveries would be treacherous for the next couple of days, but that was fine. He only had one delivery ready, and he knew that Mr. Troyer would be ready to come in on Friday to collect.

The cold took the anger away, and he was able to finish out the workday as he had originally planned. The walk had been more to enjoy the fresh air during his lunch break than to clear his head.

If he was to find a way to pay Mr. Riverton, he supposed he needed to be working as much as possible. It wouldn't be easy to make excuses to Mary but she didn't need to worry about it.

Moses walked home from the shop close to dinner time when Edna caught up to him.

"I was hoping to catch you before you went home," she said. "I've got the applications for the open teaching position. I thought you'd like to see them, check them, before I make a selection. I've highlighted the names on the applications that stood out to me, and perhaps one of them will stand out to you too."

"I'll take a look at these for you tonight, then, Edna," Moses said with a smile. "Make sure you get home safely, all right? It doesn't look like the cold is going to let up any time soon."

"Christmas is always preceded by a lot of cold and snow," she said softly. "I'll make my way home then."

"Very well."

With that, Moses started on his way home. Since it was a decent walk, and he was alone on the paths around this part of the community, he decided to take a look at the names on the applications. He'd take a more in-depth look at them once he got home, of course.

He recognized all the names, but none really stood out as the best candidate by name alone until he saw the last one on the pile. Mary's name looked up at him.

When had she applied for this position? And why would she bother? This position would go to a young, single woman in their community as it always had. Just because she had once been the teacher here didn't mean that she could do it again now that Ruth would be joining her siblings at the school *haus*.

She was a *mamm* now! This was not a *mamm's* job, to be teaching the youth in the community.

Moses could hardly contain his fury, and he shoved the applications in his pocket for the rest of the walk home.

CHAPTER 5

It had been a long day. The interview hadn't gone well, and the *kinner* had been as hyper as ever. She'd finally managed to get them to bed after a good dinner. Now that she had the dining room to herself, she was having a quiet meal alone. She'd made soup for the *familye*, and she was glad that the *kinner* hadn't been hungry enough to finish the entire pot.

There had been days when they were sick that they would do that, but today had not been one of them, thankfully.

The door opened as she was taking a sip of her soup, and she turned to see Moses coming through the door. He was visibly upset. Perhaps something had happened at work. Whatever the case, Mary decided to set the table and hope that she would be able to get him to talk to her about what had happened. Usually, when he stayed this late at the shop, he just needed a good meal to make things right.

She hoped that was all it took tonight. She could handle that.

"What's wrong, Moses?"

She put a hand on his arm as she asked this, hoping that her touch would soften his heart a little and encourage him to share what had happened at work. It had worked in the past, and so far, there hadn't been a problem that he didn't feel he could share when she did that.

He only shrugged her hand off, pushing the bowl of soup away. He was careful not to spill it, but this worried Mary. Why would he do this if he was concerned about something? Was it about the *familye*?

"Moses? Please... tell me what's wrong."

Moses folded his arms on his chest and just looked down. It was as if he was contemplating how to say what he wanted to say without screaming, which she appreciated. It was not the first time he had come home to vent to her after the *kinner* had gone to bed, but this was the first time that he had been so worked up about whatever had happened that he was struggling to find the words to tell her what had happened.

Mary sighed softly, taking her seat to resume eating her soup.

Maybe he needed some time before she started pressing for an answer as to what had happened. Whatever it was, she hoped that she would be able to entice him to open up eventually. Otherwise, there was something wrong in his eyes with something she had done, and she hated when he didn't immediately tell her what the problem was.

It always made it harder to solve, and made her feel as if she had to continually prove that she had nothing to hide at times.

She took a few sips of her soup, but he refused to say anything or even look at her. He hardly touched his soup, either.

"Has whatever happened gotten you so worked up that you cannot eat?" Mary put her spoon down. "Moses... you cannot keep it all bottled up like this. Don't freeze me out. I'm your partner. Both in happiness and in your worries."

She moved closer to him, bringing her soup with her.

"Please. If you don't want to say anything yet, at least eat something. I don't want you to go to bed with an empty stomach after I made such a delicious soup. And the *kinner* missed you at dinner. They wanted to go make snowmen with you in the yard."

Moses now scoffed at her.

"How can you believe that?" He looked at her. "Do you really believe that you're my partner in happiness and in worry?"

Mary resisted the urge to raise an eyebrow at him, but she decided he needed an answer if that was how he was going to start the discussion.

"*Jah.* I do," she said softly. "I share all my worries with you when they are there. So, what has you so worried this evening?"

He took a piece of paper out of his pocket. It had been folded and then crumpled even more. He slammed it on the dining room table.

"Then what is this?" The words came out of his mouth as a demand, not a question. Mary gulped hard. She hadn't thought that Moses would get so angry over her putting in an application to teach at the school *haus,* especially since she didn't think she was going to get the job after what happened at the interview.

"I… is that my application?"

"Edna gave them to me to look at before she made her selection," Moses continued. "I'm offended, insulted, and feel that you don't even trust me to run your plans by me. How could you do this?"

"I didn't think it was a big deal, Moses," Mary said softly. "And… I don't think I'm going to get the job anyway. The interview didn't go well."

"That won't be the only reason you don't get it," he said sharply. "I thought we agreed that you were going to do something in the *haus* to earn money and feel useful so that you could stay home with the *kinner* if you needed to while they were sick."

"I never agreed to that," Mary reminded him. "I said I would think about it, but I have dedicated my life to teaching. If I teach here in Dalton, at least I'm not taking a buggy into the city every day and taking longer to return home. By teaching here, I can still tend to all of the duties I have to the *familye.*"

Moses glared at her.

"You still have a duty to tell me what you want to do so that we can adjust our life accordingly," he spat. "By just springing this kind of thing on me, you don't make it any easier to plan for our life. I need to know what you want to do so that we can properly plan for who will take care of the *kinner.* That is your job, Mary. Taking care of

Ruth, Faith, and Elijah. A mother's place is in the home."

"And I can be a working mother once Ruth starts school," Mary argued softly. "Moses, you know how much being useful means to me. I don't want to sit around cleaning the *haus* multiple times a week just because I don't have anything else to do. Don't get me wrong, perhaps the first couple of weeks would be nice, but I can't just do that. I never wanted to be a stay-at-home *mamm.* The only reason I've delayed it this long is that Ruth hasn't been to school yet. That changes this year. Why shouldn't I be able to work outside of the home?"

"Who would take care of the *kinner* when they are sick? Or if something were to break at the *haus,* who would take care of it?"

"Moses..."

"You have no right to talk about sharing each other's burdens when this is how I find out that you don't want to work around the home," Moses said, venom lacing his voice.

He got up from the table, effectively ending the discussion. He didn't even take his bowl of soup. Something about the discussion, or about the worry, had made him lose his appetite.

She frowned as she sat down to finish her

own soup. She had lost her appetite, too, but not completely.

Once she was done with her dinner, Mary cleaned up and did the dishes. As much as she wanted to say that Moses was wrong for saying that she needed to share what she wanted to do with him, she also felt that he was wrong to say that she needed to find a way to stay home now that Ruth was going to be in school.

Why Moses didn't think it was sufficient to leave it at her not thinking the interview went well, she didn't know. She thought that he would have known better than to pick at something that she already thought hadn't gone well.

When she was done with the dishes, and they were all put away, Mary returned to the *kinner's* rooms to check in on them as they slept.

There, she found all three fast asleep. It was peaceful and quiet in the room, instead of hot-headed and angry. She knew how Moses could be when he was that angry at her, and she didn't want to push it any further by trying to snuggle with him tonight. Instead, she pulled an extra quilt and pillow from the closet in the hall.

She quietly set up a small bed on Ruth and Faith's bedroom floor. Since she would have to get up early to make breakfast, she didn't think they would notice. They all slept through the night, and usually only Ruth got up to use the bathroom in the middle of the night. Faith and Elijah didn't have to do so anymore.

As Mary lay down on the floor watching Ruth and Faith sleep, she took in a deep breath in an attempt to stifle the tears she felt burning her eyes. This was not the time and place to start crying. While Moses had his workshop, she didn't have anywhere to be alone without worrying anyone. Not while everyone was home for the holidays, anyway.

Why did Moses always have to assume that she was making things difficult when she didn't share her plans with him? She sometimes just thought that he didn't need to know because it wasn't that big a deal. Apparently, she was always wrong.

Whatever the case, she knew that she didn't want to worry her *kinner*. So, she took a deep, quiet breath as the tears were pushed down and she swallowed the lump in her throat. She'd talk to Moses tomorrow when she was calmer. It wouldn't do any good to continue having this conversation when they were both worked up and emotional.

As she closed her eyes, she listened to the

wood around her settle into place for the night. If she moved much, she would make the wood creak and settle again. She didn't want to wake her *kinner*, and honestly, if Moses wanted her to sleep in the bedroom with him, he could find her.

She wasn't even sure he would do that, but she knew that it was a possibility.

Sleep stole her eventually, taking her to the distant dreamland that allowed her to get her mind off the argument and allowing her to calm down even further.

CHAPTER 6

M oses didn't sleep well that night. He had hoped that Mary would come to bed regardless of what had been said. After all, they'd had worse arguments before about her keeping things from him, and they had always worked it out before going to bed. When he could no longer keep his eyes open because he was too tired to try, he wondered where Mary had decided to sleep.

The only place that made sense was the *kinner's* room. Or one of them, anyway. He hadn't expected her to snuggle with him, but to sleep in the room with their *dochders* or with their *sohn* instead of with him did hurt. The audacity to do that.

He didn't need *familye* problems on top of dealing with Mr. Riverton. He should have sucked it up and eaten the soup, or at least pretended that he wasn't as angry as he was. Perhaps some of his anger was boiling over due to the situation with Mr. Riverton. Regardless, it was not a good thing to worry about right now.

He could smell the breakfast cooking down the hall. The *kinner* were making a ruckus, which is what had woken him, but he wasn't angry about that. He loved waking up to the sounds of his *kinner* having a good morning. He could hear Mary calling them to the table and slowly got up out of bed. He could get ready for the workshop quickly.

Once he was ready, he walked out to find Mary plating his breakfast. However, the more he thought about it, the more he wished that she would just find a way to be content in the *haus* and stay here. She needed to be with the *kinner*, and that was the woman's job, after all. Taking care of the *kinner* wasn't a man's job. Not here.

Moses lost his appetite and didn't touch his food, but he did drink out of the glass that Mary had set down. Once the children had left the room, Mary sat down with him.

"This is absolutely ridiculous, Moses," she said

as she looked at his uneaten food. "You need to eat to do your work. I know you're angry at me over what I did, but I cannot bear to see you punishing yourself like this for my decisions."

"Then what do you call all of this?" He again motioned to the paper that had not moved from where he had slammed it down the night before. "You do not need to work! I can take care of you and the *kinner* financially. You are needed in the home to care for them physically."

"I need something else as well," Mary said softly. "Caring for the *kinner* and the *haus* is repetitive work. And with being alone at the *haus* this year, I don't know what there would be for me to do if you expect me to stay at home all day long. I cannot do that, Moses. I need more!"

"We... we aren't enough for you?"

Moses's blood ran cold at this thought.

He simply got up from the table as Mary stammered, perhaps trying to clarify her thoughts. He didn't want to hear it. Not right now. She could have all the time she needed to think about it while he was at the carpentry shop, and there was nothing he could do to stop her from thinking about it.

He just wished that she would use her head and *think* how her words affected him. He was only glad that the *kinner* had not been there to hear them fight.

As he walked the paths to work, he wondered what had gotten into Mary. She had loved staying home just a few years ago when the *kinner* were younger. Was it because she would be alone all day? Did she want another *boppli*? He would gladly give her another one if that was what she wanted because he wanted to see her happy, but he didn't understand this need to get out of the *haus* and work. He didn't expect her to stay cooped up in the *haus* all day, every day.

Upon his arrival at the shop, he shook those thoughts away.

Mr. Riverton had not shown up yet, so Moses decided that he was going to take advantage of that and shovel the little walkway up to the shop. Thankfully, only a few footprints had been pressed in and it was easy enough to dig out a path. He'd done a better job in getting a path ready for deliveries out back where no one had been walking.

As he was getting ready to open for the day, Mr. Troyer arrived.

"I know I'm a couple of days early, but by any chance do you have the rattle ready?" he questioned. "Her friend went into labor a little early, and Edna wanted to present the rattle when the *boppli* is born."

"*Jah.* And, if you brought a buggy, you can take the couch, too," Moses replied. "They're both ready when you are for them."

"Oh, that's great news," Mr. Troyer smiled widely. "I'm glad to hear it. Let's get the couch loaded up on my buggy, then. I brought it to pick up something else at another location, but that can be dealt with later."

Moses was glad for the distraction. He didn't want to believe that Mary meant what she had said, and the only way to really keep him from thinking about it was to make sure that he had something else to think about.

"Let's get it out of here before Mr. Riverton realizes there's another entrance that people are using to see me," Moses said. "I can't believe he's not yet given up the charade. I don't know how I'm going to deal with him."

"Well, you'll find a way in time," Mr. Troyer said. "The community is rallying around you, Moses. We don't like to see you get harassed like this any more than you like it."

Moses managed a smile. He was relieved to hear that the community didn't like to see him struggle. They all depended on him for advice now, and to see him getting attacked in this way probably didn't bolster their confidence.

With that, Moses shook the thoughts away. He had something else to take care of, and he was not going to let something as simple as termites get the better of him. Not today.

With Mr. Troyer's help, they were able to get the couch into Mr. Troyer's buggy. The baby rattle fit in the pocket of Mr. Troyer's jacket just as Moses had intended. In spite of everything happening with Mr. Riverton's furniture, he was happy that he was still able to provide whatever the community needed from him.

"*Danke* for your help, Moses," Mr. Troyer said. "I don't know what I would have done if you weren't in business to do this for me. I mean it."

"It's nothing." Moses managed a smile. "Go see your *familye*. Tell Edna I say *hallo*."

Mr. Troyer nodded before leaving for other parts of the community. Moses returned inside his workshop, stamping his shoes free of snow as he walked in. He didn't need to create a sliding hazard on his shop floor and cause himself or his customers a risk of injury. That would have been the worst thing to happen with Mr. Riverton threatening to have his clientele leave.

As he took his coat off to get the fire going, Moses's thoughts wondered back to the issues he was battling.

Moses shook his head.

There would be plenty of time to fix things with Mary, no matter how upset he was over what she had done or the implication that she thought he wasn't bringing enough money in to allow the *familye* to survive on his salary alone. This wasn't an *Englischer* city where they had to worry about a high cost of living, buying school uniforms, supplies, and having to buy all their food from the supermarket. They weren't on their *rumspringa*.

They had everything they needed right there. Right in that *haus*, so why couldn't Mary see it?

Once the fire was blazing in the fireplace in the workshop, he sat down to start working on a table that had been ordered. used Amann had ordered it as a surprise for his ill wife. She'd been asking for a new table for ages, and though it had taken much saving, her *mann* had finally managed to do it. He had come in all smiles to order it, knowing that his *fraa* was going to be so happy to see that they finally had a table that was theirs and not something that had been inherited from someone else.

Moses took extra care with the rose detail on the legs of the table. He had been told that the rose was this woman's favorite flower. It meant taking his time, making sure each petal was crafted well. He felt proud that this man had wanted to surprise his *fraa* in this way.

And he was an *Englischer*. Knowing how expensive *Englisch* medicine could be, thanks to witnessing Brian's hospitalization and recovery after he came out of a coma, Moses knew that this was going to be a surprise of a lifetime for this woman.

All his work came to a halt, however, when he heard Mr. Riverton shouting at the clients to leave and not to order from this crook again. Moses put the leg of the table down and went to see if he could do anything to resolve this situation. Clearly, ignoring his cries would not make him leave the shop, so he had to do something.

"Mr. Riverton? Would you like to discuss this inside, perhaps?" Moses did his best to keep his voice calm, his tone even. "I cannot have you standing out here every day until you have disrupted my business beyond repair."

"That's what you deserve, Mr. Lapp," Mr. Riverton replied sharply. "I'll continue driving your customers away until I get my refund! How dare you deliver a furniture set riddled with termites? You advertise termite-free furniture, but mine was riddled with the vermin."

"And I have offered everything I can to fix it," he said quietly. "Perhaps you could show me photos you took before you threw the furniture away?"

"I didn't stop to take photos," Mr. Riverton admitted. "I didn't want to risk the vermin getting into my house! Now, if you'll give me the refund and compensation that I've asked for…"

Moses stuttered, but ultimately went inside listening to Mr. Riverton continue to turn his customers away.

CHAPTER 7

Mary sat at the table, trying to figure out how she could resolve this argument with Moses. He was right to walk away from her after she said that she needed more, but she hadn't meant that they weren't enough for her. She needed more than looking after the *haus*. Besides, there was always going to be part of her that wanted to teach. She hadn't been able to do the same kind of teaching in the home as she had in school, and it was driving her crazy.

But for now, she needed to focus on keeping the *kinner* busy. They wanted to go out and make snow angels and snowmen. It was a beautiful day out, but she was worried they would catch a cold if they were to interact with some of the other *kinner* in the community. There was a flu going around, she'd heard. While they lived on the edge by the carpentry shop, it wasn't long before something like this hit them, too, because Moses worked with a lot of people.

She eventually decided that it would make that night easier if she let them work out whatever energy they could this morning while it was still warm and light outside. So, she got them all bundled up in their cloaks and jackets, with boots on their feet and mittens on their hands, before doing the same for herself.

Once outside, they were happy to go nuts on any of the snow they saw. Faith and Ruth ended up working together to make the body of the snowman while Elijah worked on making the middle part. Mary could only smile. At least she had done a good job teaching them how to cooperate, but she worried that they had absorbed some of the *Englisch* ways despite her not talking about it much.

There were times when they competed with each other to see who could roll the largest snowball, and who could do their best to make the deepest snow angel when they'd had a fresh snowfall. It wasn't the worst kind of competition, as eventually they would all end up working together anyway, but she had seen Moses's lips pucker when they worked like that: competition, then cooperation.

Despite it all, Moses had been the one to ask her to help to make sure that all the *kinner* in the community were ready for their *rumspringa*. Had he not expected that she would prepare their *kinner* in the same manner that she had helped prep others?

The morning spent outside was fun to watch, and when they all went inside to dry off and warm up, the *kinner* had worked together to build one giant snowman and had all built little snowmen around him. It was a beautiful sight.

However, Mary got no rest as it was time to make lunch. She made simple sandwiches before getting to work on a stew for dinner. She wanted soup, but she'd made that the night before and there had been none left over.

When Moses arrived home for dinner, it was quiet. The *kinner* picked up on the quiet tension and did their best not to be disruptive. She hated seeing them exchange awkward glances to see who had finished and when they were all done, they excused themselves and went up to their rooms to play. Probably to play in Elijah's room.

It would give her the time she needed to talk to her *mann*.

"Moses... you were right. It was wrong of me to apply for the teaching position without telling you that I was planning to do so," Mary said in as calm and even voice as she could manage. "However, I need to get out of the *haus* to feel whole again. I love being your *fraa*, being a *mamm*, but there is also a part of me that needs to teach. That's not going to go away. You originally brought me to Dalton all those years ago to teach... and I want to keep doing that."

Moses pursed his lips and then spoke, almost without thinking. "You don't know how hard it is to make a living here," he said sarcastically.

Mary bit her tongue for a moment. She knew that he was probably right, but only because no one had let her try. Even when she had been teaching Edna and Elise how to teach the values of the *Englisch,* she had been staying in the lodging *haus* on money she had earned. The Dalton contract hadn't been worth much, which is why she had originally been sent. Good teaching on a budget.

"Try me. Maybe you'll see that what I do is also rather tough, despite your depiction," Mary eventually replied. "I am home all day, and there are things I want to do that I simply can't while I am watching the *kinner*."

Moses raised an eyebrow before leaning in a little. This intrigued Mary. He only did this when he was about to say something he wanted her to pay attention to, and she wondered what it could be this time. Certainly, he wasn't about to tell her that the teaching position had already been filled... was he?

"Perhaps you're right." He leaned back in his chair. "I do not see what you do all day long, but you take care of the *kinner*. And I see what they are like at home with the two of us. It cannot be *that* difficult to take care of them without any prior experience."

It took everything in Mary not to laugh.

She knew that Moses was only trying to be the proper kind of *mann* that the Amish community could look up to, but she knew that he was in for quite a surprise when he found that her job at home was harder than it looked. He wondered why she no longer had the energy for intimacy while the reasons behind his lack of attentiveness were more obvious. He was the one with a full-time job out of the *haus* as well as having to deal with the community's problems as the elder. She couldn't help but think that most of her issues were invisible to anyone who was not involved in the full-time work she had been doing for eight years now.

"How long do we switch for, then, if you think you can handle it?"

"I think a week should do just fine," Moses replied. "You will watch the shop for a week, and I will watch the *kinner* for a week. Perhaps it will help us both remember in the future what the other goes through on a daily basis when we want to pick a fight about doing things other than what the community agrees is proper for a *familye*."

Mary nodded.

As much as she wanted to point out that just because the community deemed it right for a *familye* to act in a specific way, didn't make it the only way for anyone to act within their role. Then again, she supposed that was a very *Englisch* way of thinking about it. So was their way of approaching the problem, but no one could argue with it since it was Moses's idea.

Mary held her hand out for him to shake.

"Then we shake on it. Make it a proper agreement, as any other agreement in this community is made," she said. "And we start tomorrow."

He nodded, shaking her hand.

"I'm sorry for walking out this morning," Moses said as he leaned back after shaking her hand. "Sometimes, it is hard to hear how the situation is affecting you, regardless of how well thought out it is when you say it. When you blurted out that you needed more, I was so hurt, but I am glad to see that it is not an entirely impossible thing to fulfill. I must ask, though: why does teaching our *kinner* not fulfill that need to teach? I would have thought that that would fill your need to be a teacher."

"So would I, but I think there is something that cannot be replaced at home in a school system, even if it is a single room school *haus*," Mary said. "A room full of *kinner* to teach is less personal than teaching only my *kinner*."

It felt like a bit of a reach as she spoke, but there was some truth to it. She simply wasn't sure what exactly it was about the environment of a classroom that fulfilled the need to teach others better than teaching her *kinner* at home. Perhaps it was because when she had been younger, she had never quite seen herself as a stay-at-home mother.

Now that that was her entire identity, she wondered if she was fighting to reclaim part of that separately from the things that a *mamm* should do in the Amish home.

Mary and Moses took their empty bowls to the kitchen, and Moses then prepared to wash the dishes.

"You've had a hard enough day. Let me start a little early. Go play with the *kinner,* and see how they're coping after all of that," Moses said softly. "I could tell they were all a little anxious during dinner. Makes me sad to know that they could tell that we were fighting and didn't want to be there for longer than needed."

Mary smiled a little at her husband.

"All right. You know where everything is to make sure everything gets scrubbed up properly. If you need my help, you know where I'll be, too," she said.

With that, she gave him a soft kiss on the cheek. He stopped her before she could pull away and gave her a kiss on the forehead, his lips only staying on her forehead for a few seconds before he pulled away.

When she walked away, she heard the sloshing of water which meant that he was getting right to work on the hardest dishes. That was always a solid method.

She found the *kinner* playing in Elijah's room,

as she had expected they would be. She smiled when they all turned to her with their wooden toys in hand.

"Do you want to play with us, *Mamm*?" Elijah looked up with wide eyes, a sparkle to them that meant that he was glad to see her happy again.

"I'd love to play, Elijah," she said as she got down on the floor. "Do you have any toys I can borrow?"

She didn't mind getting down on the floor and playing with her *kinner,* and as they told her the story they had decided to act out tonight – Daniel in the lion's den, to her surprise – she wished that Moses had come up with her for a few moments. He had the greatest growl for a lion ever, and the *kinner* all looked a little sad that she couldn't do it as well as he could when she tried.

"I'm afraid I can't do it as well as your *daed* can," Mary said when Ruth pouted at her. "But I'm doing my best to give you a good lion roar. Perhaps when he's done in the kitchen, he could come join us and give you all a good roar before you go to bed?"

"I'd like that!" Ruth immediately perked up.

As did Faith and Elijah. They were all more than happy to hear that their *daed* might be willing to come in once he was done, and Mary excused herself for much-needed water after her attempts at roaring for them.

It always made her throat itch to roar like that.

When Moses saw her coming in for water, he raised an eyebrow. Perhaps a *familye* reading of Daniel in the lions' den was in order tonight after all.

CHAPTER 8

The next morning, Mary and Moses both got up at the same time as usual. However, Moses went to cook breakfast while Mary tucked the stray hairs into her prayer *Kapp*. She wanted to at least look presentable this morning, even if she didn't stay that way after a hard day's work in the carpentry shop. She was suddenly glad that she had started learning carpentry from Moses while she had been home.

Her work might not have been nearly as good as Moses's, but it would have to do for the week.

Breakfast was passable, since Moses had been making breakfast for himself before he courted her. It wasn't quite what she might have made,

GRACE LEWIS

but she reminded herself that it was not worth it to pass judgment on what he was doing. This was not his daily routine, and as long as the *kinner* were getting fed and nourished properly, she wasn't going to give him a hard time about cooking.

It was how he behaved when the *kinner* pushed him to his limits later today that would truly be a testament to how hard parenting was when one was around the *kinner* all day, without any breaks.

Mary ate quietly. Her eggs were warm and thoroughly cooked, and the bacon was crispy. Cooked to perfection. It was one of the few things she thought he made better than she did.

"I'll see you all when I get home," Mary said. "I'll be home later tonight."

The *kinner* all looked up at her from their plates, all showing some form of shock.

"But *Mamm*... you're supposed to help us make snowmen today!" Ruth whined.

"Your *daed* is plenty capable of that," Mary reminded them. "I'll see you all when I return. Come, give me hugs. I won't be gone for the entire day, but a good majority of it."

She gave them all tight hugs, knowing this

was going to be as hard on them as it would be on her. Though she had agreed with Moses, she found herself wishing she were staying home for just a little longer. Perhaps Moses felt the same way each morning but pushed it down knowing that he would be returning each evening.

"All right. See you when you return home, Mary," Moses said with a smile as he hugged her.

He pressed a soft kiss to her cheek before letting her go.

Mary decided to walk to the carpentry shop. It wasn't too far from their *haus*, which she was always thankful for.

The scene awaiting her shocked her and that was with her having believed that she had seen enough stuck-up, entitled behavior in her time before coming to Dalton to last the rest of her lifetime.

An *Englisch* man stood at the door, yelling at the people that were trying to come in to put in their orders now that she was here to open the shop. He was yelling about Moses being a cheat for refusing to give him a refund.

Why hadn't Moses mentioned this to her before?

"Can I help you, sir?" Mary asked, managing

to keep herself from stuttering, but she already felt flustered. "Beyond looking into the situation, I mean, of course. I just… I…"

The man laughed.

"Moses is lucky that his wife is here to save him. Not everyone can hide behind a woman's skirt when the going gets tough," the man said. "Mr. Riverton, at your disservice. Your husband sold me a furniture set riddled with termites and refuses to compensate me as I have asked. Here are the calculations from my lawyer, and if I don't see the compensation soon, you can be sure that you'll be seeing a court summons for a lawsuit."

Mary gulped hard. She'd seen other small businesses destroyed by these very tactics when she was in Chicago and in other cities when still working as an *Englisch* teacher trainer. If they weren't careful, they could become destitute.

"I'll look into it and see what I can do for you, Mr. Riverton," Mary managed to say. "In the meantime if you could move along? You're blocking the door to the business."

Mr. Riverton appeared to have been unprepared for her to speak to him like this. She quietly thanked the heavens for her time as an *Englischer* herself and then quietly opened the business for the day. This was not going to be an easy thing to get ahead of and she wondered if Moses had purposefully not mentioned it to her to keep her from feeling anxious over what was going on.

The first thing she did was to look into Moses's accounts and see if it was even possible to pay this man what he was asking. It appeared, from what Mr. Riverton had told her, that he was asking for thousands in damages and compensations. She knew that Moses had been making more money off his carpentry work recently, but she didn't believe that he had been making enough to afford this payment.

And she knew that there was no insurance among the community. It was something that the Amish saw as a frivolity that was not necessary for their businesses. As much as she hated to say 'I told you so' to her husband, she had a feeling this would have been a perfect case for their insurance to handle if they had any.

Instead, the books confirmed her fears. There was not nearly enough money coming into the business to cover the business expenses *and* the damages and compensation that Mr. Riverton was demanding.

Whatever Moses's motives were for not

telling her about this problem, she knew that something had to be done soon or they would lose the shop. Without the shop, they would have no way of caring for their *kinner*, and it would ruin Moses's reputation of being a good elder to the community.

She knew how much pride he had in being the one to give the community the advice they sought. Though pride was often seen as a bad thing in Dalton, this was something different. It was just enough to make sure that he could do a good job. No one seemed to have a problem as long as it didn't become *hochmut* and become the downfall of a good *mann*, Mary didn't have a problem with Moses taking pride in his work with the community, either.

She decided to approach the books when the shop itself wasn't busy. Perhaps she could find ways to save money without causing issues with the quality, or they could start charging for delivering pieces out to the *Englischer* town. Either way, they might be able to find a way to make it work.

However, what really bugged her was that Mr. Riverton refused to show any proof that he had disposed of the furniture. Of course, she hadn't asked, but she knew that Moses would have requested a look before looking into the matter any further.

The thought of proof of the termites played in the back of her head as she helped other customers through the day. Most were customers that she knew from the community, and she was able to assure them that the quality wouldn't be affected because she was the one running the shop today.

The other *Englisch* customers who came were more interested in seeing what a proper Amish carpentry shop looked like. Some asked for Moses by name which made Mary think that perhaps they were some of the students that he had once taught years ago when he subbed for the shop teacher in the nearby *English* school.

On her lunch break, one of the other *English* business owners came in and shared a lunch with her.

"Oh, you must be Mary," he said. "I'm Jackson. Moses often speaks highly of you. Where is Moses, anyway? We usually have lunch together on Mondays."

"He's at home with the *kinner*," Mary replied. "Long story, but I'm here filling in today. Please, have a seat. I'd be more than happy to continue the tradition if you do not mind."

"Not at all."

Jackson sat down, and as they were starting to eat, Mr. Riverton's chant started up again. It was the same one that had been screamed when Mary had arrived. Moses was not a cheat, but that did not appear to stop Mr. Riverton from *trying* to dissuade people from coming to the shop. The joke was currently on him; the shop was empty and she knew that no one else would be coming for the time being.

"I can't believe he's still out there," Jackson said, shaking his head as he took a sandwich out of his lunchbox. "Wants Moses to refund him for the furniture but won't return the furniture. It's a real mind-boggler."

"The entitlement of some *Englischers* is entirely mind-boggling, in my opinion," Mary replied.

She didn't want to think about Mr. Riverton. Instead, she got to know Jackson and learned that he was in the same area as the shop. Moses hadn't wanted his shop to be so close to the edge of Dalton, but it had ended up working out in his favor.

Jackson had been in the storefront since he was a child; it had been his father's store then, but unfortunate circumstances had forced a change in ownership. He was glad to see that Mr.

Riverton's chant outside had not aroused any anxiety.

The rest of the day was rather uneventful in the shop, thankfully. It left Mary time to think about an approach to the problem that Mr. Riverton presented. She had a feeling that Moses had already asked to replace the pieces because he'd gladly do twice the work for the same price if it meant a happy customer. However, some *Englischers* were only happy if they could have their money back, regardless of the store's actual policies.

The *Englischers* needed to double-check store policy before they bought, in her opinion, but she had no way to make that happen.

It wasn't until she was getting ready to close up shop that something else happened to upset her. She had put the key in the lock to lock up for the night but it had snapped off in the lock. Unlocked. This meant they needed both a new key and a way to get the rest of the key out of the lock, otherwise, they'd have to replace the entire lock.

Mary groaned.

"That's just great..."

She let out a soft sigh as she debated what to do next.

"Are you having trouble with the lock? I've seen Moses have trouble in the winter before."

Jackson's voice startled her.

"What are you doing here, Jackson? I thought you would have left already, being an *Englisch* business owner and having different hours."

"I usually end up heading home the same time as your husband," Jackson admitted. "I stay about an extra hour to do the clean-up and closing procedures myself because I want to know that they've been done properly. Oh... well... *that's* an issue."

He pointed to the key.

She only nodded.

"I'll have to look into how to replace it tomorrow," she said. "For now, I think making it look as though it's locked will be enough."

Jackson nodded.

"Then, perhaps a walk back to where I parked? Moses usually ends up walking some of the way with me, since I have to park in an odd place."

"I think I'd rather walk alone tonight, but *danke*," Mary said. "I'm not even sure we should have had lunch together, but I wanted to see how Moses spends his day."

Jackson nodded, but then held up his phone.

"I have something I wanted to show Moses, but perhaps you'd be able to make more sense of it."

Mary raised an eyebrow and then nodded. Perhaps something good would come of today after all.

CHAPTER 9

Moses wondered how in the world Mary did this every day, all day long. The twins had no sense of calm, and it was only lunchtime. He'd already had to pull them from the barn loft twice this morning, and he worried that he'd have to do it again at least once more before Mary returned home.

Lunch was also an interesting spectacle. Faith and Elijah had eaten everything quietly, happily. But Ruth had decided that she didn't want anything that was on her plate. She'd held one bite of the food in her mouth for at least half an hour, refusing to either swallow it or spit it out. She didn't want to eat anything else on her plate and was making the only "good food" last as long as she could.

Moses wasn't sure when Ruth had developed such a narrow palette, but he wondered how in the world Mary dealt with this. Ruth needed to eat more. Considering he'd seen her finish her plate before, he knew that Mary had a method that worked. He should have asked what it was before agreeing to watch the *kinner* for a full week.

As it was, he was on his own for lunch. He knew that she'd eat what he cooked for breakfast since it was a smaller version of Mary's breakfasts. Dinner would be a struggle, especially since he had a feeling that Mary was not going to pick up any of the slack when she got home from the carpentry shop. Why should she? They had switched jobs for the full week.

And it was his job to get Ruth to eat lunch.

She did eventually swallow when her lunch was clearly going to go to waste.

"Ruth?" Moses pulled her aside when Faith and Elijah went to get ready for their naps. They'd been playing outside all morning, and he was glad that they had been able to tire themselves out. He needed a break, as much as he hated to admit it.

"*Jah?*"

"I don't want to see you hungry after dinner tonight," Moses said softly. "I know it's hard to adjust to a different schedule, but your *Mamm* has other duties to take care of today. Can you try to eat your dinner for me? Instead of allowing the food to sit there and go to waste, I'd appreciate it if you could eat it."

Ruth only nodded.

He wasn't sure this was actually going to work, but it was worth a shot. With her nod, he sent her to her room for a nap.

As the *haus* fell quiet, Moses took in a deep breath. He hadn't realized how much he missed the intellectual stimulation until now. However, he had to clean the *haus* first.

It didn't take long since they had been outside for much of the morning. Trying to wash the dishes quietly was difficult, but as long as he didn't intentionally drop any of the dishes, he figured he would be fine.

Once the whole home was tidied, which didn't take nearly as long as he thought it might have since the *kinner* were not making trouble or making more of a mess, he realized how much he wanted to take a walk or meet with other adults. But he couldn't. The *kinner* would wake up eventually, and he needed to be here when they did.

As he sat in the living room, the quiet speaking volumes around him, he had to wonder how Mary did this with a smile on her face, day in and day out. It was a never-ending cycle of things to do, and he was already exhausted after one day.

He shook his head.

Perhaps he had been too quick to discount what Mary did when the *kinner* were home all day. She did have at least one point when it came to the benefits of the teaching job here in Dalton over one in the *Englisch* town: she would be home with their *kinner* when they were out of school.

Moses knew that he wouldn't be able to continue to care for them like this when he had to return to the shop. He already had hardly enough time to take care of everything that required his attention when he was home after a full day at the shop, and that was without the entitled *Englischers* demanding that he refund them for furniture they weren't going to return because they'd already thrown it out.

Despite wanting to leave home and take a walk to meet with other adults, Moses realized there was something he could do while the *kinner* were asleep that wouldn't require him to leave or risk waking them up. He could start on dinner. It would be difficult, nigh impossible, to get it started once they woke up.

Moses decided that he was going to make a simple soup for dinner. He wondered if this was why they always had soups and such in the winter; it was something that Mary could easily make while the *kinner* were asleep but that she didn't have to watch as closely as some of the other dishes she loved to make.

He pulled out the large stockpot and poured in water and broth.

He'd have to apologize to Mary when this was all over. It was already too much for him, and he wondered how she was getting along at the shop. If he was starting to feel like he had taken on too much, was it possible that she would feel the same way once she realized what he hid so that she didn't feel like she had to be earning money too?

As the soup simmered, and the meat and vegetables cooked, Moses sat down at the dining room table. His eyes drooped, and he allowed himself to close them for a few seconds since he had been running on little food all day.

Then he realized that he could do something

else. He might have had dinner cooking, but it was still a good couple of hours before dinner time. He didn't think he'd make it that long without eating. With the *kinner* asleep, he could get a quick bite to eat that wasn't a cold sandwich.

"Let's toast a slice of bread and have something warm today," Moses whispered as he heated a secondary pan to toast the bread. While a toaster might have been of help here, he was glad that he didn't have one.

Mary arrived home a little later than he had thought she would. Perhaps she had lost track of time. Regardless, dinner was on the table and ready when she got home even if it wasn't the best soup in the world. The *kinner* had woken up about half an hour before she arrived home, and he thanked the heavens that he had prepared dinner before they woke up.

"I'm glad to see that everything's all right here," Mary said as she walked in and took her cloak off. "I was wondering how you did today. How are you three?" She looked to the *kinner* who were now swarming her instead of paying attention to their food.

Considering that is what happened when he arrived home, he couldn't fault Mary for giving them all a hug before escorting them back to the table. Her eyes betrayed her exhaustion, but Moses didn't say anything about it. Mary said nothing of how exhausted he must have looked when he returned home, nor how exhausted he felt right now, so he was going to extend her the same courtesy.

"Moses, this smells delicious. *Danke* for making dinner tonight, too," Mary said.

Moses's heart stung momentarily. He rarely thanked her anymore for making dinner, perhaps because he had gotten so used to the fact that it would be ready when he got home because it was part of her job. Or perhaps he had forgotten that he used to do that when it was just the two of them until tonight.

He quietly resolved that he was going to do better.

She may not have had as easy a job as he had originally thought, and she deserved all of the thanks he could give her for handling it so well compared to how he had thought she was handling it. Having a smile on her face every day as she dealt with the mischief that his *kinner* could get up to at times required real skill.

And she deserved to be thanked for it.

Thankfully, she helped with the bedtime routine as they usually did that together. They fell into their usual routine for it, which was nice for Moses. It was a brief moment of normality, something that he could handle while Mary took care of the hardest part of the bedtime routine.

Alone in their room while the *kinner* were getting ready for bed in their rooms, Mary was getting ready for bed while Moses was getting ready to snuggle under the covers with her.

"How was your day?" Moses didn't know how else to broach the topic, and he knew that it needed to be asked.

He knew that Mr. Riverton had probably given Mary a hard time today, but he wasn't sure if she was going to share what had happened. If she did, he knew that she was probably going to ask if he'd had just as hard a time with her job as she had with his.

She turned around and gave him a bright smile.

"It was a great day," she said brightly, matching her smile. "Lots of customers."

Moses wanted to raise an eyebrow but managed to resist. He knew Mr. Riverton would not stop until his business was destroyed, or he had given a refund, so this must have been a lie to show that she could handle what she was seeing.

98

"How about your day?" Mary continued speaking as she walked towards the bed. "Were the *kinner* well behaved for you?"

"They were *Wunderbar*," he lied with as bright a smile as he could muster. "It was as easy as I thought it would be. I must not understand why you want to get out of the *haus*, but perhaps if they were in school all day long, I'd understand where you were coming from."

She nodded slowly.

"Well, then, we continue with this tomorrow," she said. "And we should probably get to bed early. I'm exhausted. I might have had a good day, but it was exhausting. That much, I cannot lie about. I feel like I'm going to fall asleep standing up. Do you always feel like that?"

"Depends on how much I have to make that day," Moses admitted. "But you're lucky I've taken care of most of the orders that have come in lately. You'll have to work on some yourself this week."

"I did some carpentry work today," she said softly. "My arms are going to be so sore tomorrow. How do you do this day in and day out?"

"That part, I believe, is just because I've been doing carpentry for years on end," Moses said. "My arms were sore like that when I first started.

99

It's going to get easier, but I don't know that you have the time to put into it to make it easier in that manner."

Mary sighed as she climbed into bed and pressed a kiss to his cheek.

"Whatever we end up doing, I think I do not envy the way your muscles must hurt at the end of each day," she said.

He pulled her close and held her as she quickly fell asleep.

CHAPTER 10

Today, Mary walked to the carpentry shop with a determined pep in her step. After talking to Jackson yesterday, she believed she had something that she could use to get Mr. Riverton to drop his rebellion outside the shop. She wasn't sure if Moses had been aware of it, or if Jackson had not yet had the chance to show him, but she was glad that she was taking care of the shop for the week.

Otherwise, Jackson would have had to share this twice, and Moses may not have known what to do with the evidence that he had found.

Upon arrival at the shop, Mary was glad to see that she had managed to arrive early enough to allow her to open without any issues. No customers were waiting for her to open, and Mr. Riverton had not yet arrived to heckle those who still wanted Amish quality furniture at a good price.

Mary decided that she was going to tackle some of the smaller orders while she waited for customers to arrive. There were plenty of baby rattles on the list, as well as a small cradle for a *boppli*, that had been ordered. She wondered if there was a craze going on in the *Englisch* town nearby, as most of these items were to be sent out after they were finished.

She looked through the paperwork to check the information Moses had taken down when he took these orders. With the rattles, most of the customers didn't know the gender of their unborn *boppli*. Those who knew had informed Moses accordingly and he had made a note.

Mary smiled a little.

Two of the *familyes* were having girls, and one was having a little boy. Since she knew what this meant to the *familyes*, she decided that she was going to do something a little special for them. For the *familyes* having girls, she fashioned two rattles that were shaped more like a crown or tiara, but she wasn't quite sure how yet and she didn't have the necessary experience to further clarify it with detail work. And the *familye* having the boy got an elephant.

The rest of the *familyes* got circular, nonspecific rattles.

As she was working on carving the elephant's trunk, something that needed precise details and concentration, she heard shouting outside. Instead of risking the structure of the rattle, she set it down. Moses might have been able to work through this, but it was actually what Mary had been waiting for.

Instead of ignoring Mr. Riverton and hoping that he went away, Mary was going to take a very *Englisch* approach to making sure that he didn't bother the shop again. Moses might not agree with it, but he wasn't here to take care of the problem. And he didn't have the contacts necessary for this to sound as threatening as it needed to.

Especially since he had decided that he was going to hide the problem from her instead of telling her what was going on as soon as it started.

"Moses Lapp is a cheat and a weak man who hides behind his wife's skirts when he's in trouble. You'd be better off spending your money anywhere else!" Mr. Riverton yelled. "How can you trust a man who says he will sell you wonderful furniture, only for there to be *termites* in everything? The simple answer is that you cannot."

Mary's heart ran cold at these words, but she took a deep breath. This was only ever going to get fixed if she was able to stay on target.

The first thing she did was leave through the back door from which Moses dispatched the orders for delivery, and made her way to Jackson to pay him a visit.

"What can I do for you this morning, Mary?" Jackson looked up from his cash register. "I can hear him yelling from here, by the way. He's going to drive away all of the customers if you don't do something. Or have Moses do something. I know you're not going to be able to pay him everything he wants upfront, but surely you could come to an agreement about some kind of payment plan?"

"If I give him a payment plan, it will only encourage others like him to come out of the woodwork, if you'll excuse the metaphor," Mary said with a sigh. "Do you mind if I borrow your phone? I think I have an idea. If it gets him to go away, I'll owe you a favor. Or Moses might, depending. I'll talk to him about it."

"If it gets Mr. Riverton out of the neighborhood, you'll have done all the shops here a favor. We're sick of him."

Jackson handed his phone over to her after fiddling with it for a moment.

"I trust that you're going to use it for only one purpose, so I've taken the passcode off. That keeps my passcode safe for when you return it."

"That's very generous of you," Mary said softly. *Danke.* Now, let's see what I can do with this, shall we?"

Jackson gave her a quizzical look but nodded all the same. If he wanted to see what was going to happen, he'd have to step outside his shop. Regardless, she wasn't going to stop him from watching this confrontation.

It was probably going to be the talk of the little shopping plaza when she was done. She'd seen others struggling to continue with business as usual because of Mr. Riverton's yelling at the front door of her husband's shop. How could Moses decide that ignoring the problem would make it go away? Or had he been attempting to find ways to pay him off to make him go away, not knowing that it would bring more leeches like Mr. Riverton to the shop to bleed him dry?

Mr. Riverton caught sight of her as she

walked out of Jackson's shop. She only offered a soft smile.

That was exactly what she had been hoping would happen.

"And here she is, the wife! Where is your husband, or is he too afraid to face me and make this better like a proper man should?" Mr. Riverton sneered. "Or have you come to tell me that you're going to pay me and this is all going to go away?"

"I'm sorry, Mr. Riverton, but the reason it's taken so long to address this situation is because there's a conduct here in Dalton that you've violated and my husband wasn't sure how to address it," Mary started. "Let's start with this: where is the furniture, Mr. Riverton? What have you done with the termite-infested wooden pieces?"

"I no longer have it," he said. "What? Was I supposed to risk the termites spreading throughout my house until such time as you rectified the matter?"

"*Nee,* but we cannot give you a refund or pay you damages unless I can see the furniture. So you may simply have to absorb the cost of the furniture as the price of doing business and know better for next time. However, if you were to find photos of the infestation or the furniture, we could address the situation a little more fairly for everyone involved."

"I don't lie," Mr. Riverton snapped. "And I thought the Amish didn't approve of the use of cameras. Why would I have kept the furniture to infest someone's place of work by bringing it back?"

Mary had to admit that Mr. Riverton had thought of everything. However, she didn't allow this to deter her. She pulled out Jackson's phone and opened the browser app that he had shown her the day before.

"You see, Mr. Riverton, I was not always an Amish woman," Mary said. "You wouldn't know it from looking me, I know, but I have an awareness about the dealings of people like you that my husband doesn't. Not everyone is honest in their dealings in the city. It's a lesson I've learned the hard way. So you can imagine my surprise when another business owner showed me this photo."

She turned the phone screen to show the image to Mr. Riverton.

His face paled.

"The photos and date on your social media page show that the furniture is still in your *haus* as of last night and that you're enjoying the use of the furniture." Mary looked Mr. Riverton square in the eye as she continued, "Now that we have established that you have no cause and no reason to expect either a refund or damages, I'd like to make one thing very clear: I do not tolerate people trying to make my husband look like a fool. If you do not leave this good Amish business alone, as well as the rest of us here trying to make our living in a quiet, peaceful manner, I will file a case against you for slander."

"You wouldn't get anywhere without a lawyer."

Mr. Riverton attempted to remain in control of the situation, perhaps because there was now a crowd watching them.

"That is where you are wrong, Mr. Riverton. My *bruder* is a lawyer, and I know that he would be more than happy to represent me in court if I were to explain the situation. With Moses's word and the word of the rest of the business owners here, I suppose that there would be a judge hard-pressed to find you innocent."

Mr. Riverton didn't even respond. He simply looked from her to the crowd, and then decided the best course of action was to run clear through the crowd.

Mary let him. She didn't need to run after him to make sure that her message came across as clear as day. The fact that he was running made her rather sure that he had not expected her to know what to do. Had he only been dealing with Moses, he might have been able to get away with it.

As she walked back towards Jackson's shop, she felt a sense of pride in her ability to problem solve. It may not have been the only thing she had to do today, but it was certainly the best thing she had done today so far.

She handed the phone back to Jackson.

"*Danke* for allowing me to borrow it for a few minutes," Mary said. "I think the results speak for themselves. I doubt Mr. Riverton will be back to harass any of the businesses around here. If he is, he ought to know to follow the refund policies to the letter this time around."

Jackson nodded.

"I've never seen an Amish business take such a stance against a greedy man, and I'm glad I could help you do that," he said. "Color me impressed. He didn't seem all that scared of you *or* Moses when he first started his campaign to smear the store, but by the end of that little talk with you, I could see the fear in his eyes. And you didn't say anything that wasn't true."

"That, and it's not illegal to threaten to take

someone to court, which is why he was using that particular threat to extort the money from Moses," Mary assumed. "But that's all I can do with that. I should be getting back to the shop. I probably have customers who are thrilled that they'll be able to place an order without having to worry about getting past him now."

Jackson smiled and went back inside his shop. Mary returned to the carpentry shop, where she continued to work on the baby rattles. Moses could make a few of these in a day, but she had been struggling to get the circular shape just right. That and the elephant's trunk on the baby boy's rattle.

She was sure their *sohn* would love it; Moses had made a rattle like this for Elijah when he was born.

CHAPTER 11

Two days. That's all he had spent with the *kinner* full-time, and Moses was already ready for this week to end. Mary must have had a lot more patience than he had ever thought, because he was doing his best not to yell at the *kinner* amidst the havoc. It didn't help that they didn't appear to be taking him seriously, and he doubted that Mary would have made his job harder by telling them not to listen to him.

Perhaps he needed to be spending more time with them at home instead of taking care of the other chores that Mary tended to.

Right now, Elijah and Faith were making a mess of the kitchen. Ruth was pulling all of the clothing out of Mary's dresser in an effort to "look like *Mamm*," which Moses didn't understand at all. How could Ruth make such a mess on her own, while Faith and Elijah had made as much of a mess together?

It didn't help that because he was trying to get everything cleaned up, the stew for dinner was on high heat burning on the stove, which was meant to be on simmer by now, or that the laundry had been sitting in the washtub water for about an hour.

"Faith, Elijah, please, I need to make dinner and this mess is not helping," Moses pleaded. "Can you two go get Ruth out of my bedroom and clean up in here?"

"But *Daed*, we're making flour angels!" Faith whined.

They had dumped the bag of flour on the floor and were using it like snow. While he understood the appeal of snow that didn't melt or make one cold, Moses was now worried about how they would afford to replace so much flour with Mr. Riverton still threatening the shop. He doubted that Mary would be able to find a way to curb his harassment while he was here with the *kinner*, but he didn't doubt that she would try her best to solve the problem as best she could.

He took the stew off the stove and managed to

make it past his two older *kinner*. However, as he was trying to salvage it, he could tell that this had been burnt past any point of salvation. Could Mary have saved it? She probably would not have burnt it in the first place.

If Mary were to see this, what would she say? Would she scold him for burning not only the dinner but the pot as well?

He sighed and set it aside so that he could deal with it when it cooled down. He hated to have to start over, but now it looked like he'd have to make cold sandwiches.

"Faith! Elijah! I need you out of the kitchen," Moses said sternly.

He managed to keep his voice even, surprisingly, but they still did not listen to him.

He sighed softly. Mary was meant to be coming home soon. Perhaps she could offer him tips if she wanted to continue to go to the store for the rest of the week. Because this was not equitable.

The door opened while he was thinking what to say to Mary, and when he looked over, he was more than happy to see Mary standing in the doorway. Her eyes had opened wide, and her mouth fell slack in shock.

He simply raised his hands in defeat.

"I surrender, Mary," he said as he walked towards her. "I give up."

Mary actually laughed.

"Wasn't so easy, now, was it?" She walked over as she asked this before giving him a kiss on his cheek.

Then, as if she were some sort of magician, she clapped her hands. This caused Faith and Elijah to look up from the flour they were playing in, and Ruth came running out of their bedroom with one of Mary's prayer *kapps* on her head.

"It's bath time," Mary said. "Especially for you, Faith, and Elijah. Hurry along."

"*Jah, Mamm!*"

With that, the three *kinner* hurried along to their bathtub. Mary grabbed a pot from underneath the sink to fill with water, and then looked at Moses' attempt at a stew.

"I burnt it rather badly," he admitted. "I'm not sure it can be salvaged. But the pot can be."

"At least the pot is okay," she said softly. "Moses... I think after we get the *kinner* to bed, we need to have a talk about the last couple of days. You need to go back to the shop, don't you?"

"I was hoping you wouldn't mind if that was what happened, but you're right. This is a better topic to be discussed once the *kinner* are in bed. Where do you want me for now?"

"Do you think you could clean up the laundry? I can see it in the washtub."

"I can finish the laundry," Moses said. "I was in the middle of doing it during their nap and trying to keep an eye on dinner and… it didn't end well."

"I can tell," Mary said with a laugh. "But for now, help out around the *haus*. I'll take care of getting the *kinner* bathed and fed."

Moses nodded and returned to the laundry that had been left soaking for too long. He added a little more of the soap, and then started rinsing the suds out of the clothing. Once they were no longer dripping wet, he was able to get them all hung up to dry in front of the fireplace. It was far too cold to dry them outside; he didn't want to freeze any of the clothing accidentally.

Mary returned shortly after getting the bath water heated up for the *kinner* and started on a proper dinner.

"Do you have any leftovers that didn't get used in the stew, Moses?" Mary looked over at him as he finished pinning the last apron up on the line.

"*Jah*. Here, let me get it for you," he said softly.

He walked into the kitchen and grabbed all

the things that he had used as well as all he had saved for another night.

"I'm sorry to waste so much of the food."

"We all burn things occasionally, Moses," she said. "The important thing is that you were able to keep the *haus* from burning down, or allowing the *kinner* to get hurt. I'd rather have burnt food than a sobbing child with burns."

Moses nodded. That was why he had been doing his best to get Faith and Elijah out of the kitchen. He didn't understand why they hadn't wanted to leave, but this was not the time to bring it up.

Mary made a quick vegetable stew, not wanting to use more meat because the *kinner* needed to get to bed soon.

"What is with the flour on the floor? It looks like they dumped an entire bag out." Mary frowned as she started sweeping it up.

Little clouds of flour met her with every movement she made with the broom, but she was not fazed by anything that was going on.

"Faith and Elijah decided that it would be fun to make flour angels since I couldn't watch them make snow angels outside and make dinner at the same time," Moses admitted. "Ruth was in the bedroom pulling all your clothing out of the dresser. Perhaps I should go tidy that before dinner is finished."

"That would be helpful if you could."

Moses nodded and headed into the bedroom.

It didn't take him long to get the bedroom back in order, but he was amazed at how destructive Ruth could be when left to her own devices. It took both Faith and Elijah to do the same amount of emptying when Ruth was doing it all on her own.

Once Mary's clothing was properly folded and returned to their drawers, Moses made sure that all of his clothing was properly stored, too. Oddly enough, Ruth had not touched his clothing. Perhaps it was because Ruth had wanted to be like her *mamm* tonight and had been trying to find clothing that would allow her to look like Mary.

Ruth wore the same clothing as Mary's, only of a different size and without a prayer *Kapp* and an apron. Perhaps it was the prayer *Kapp* that had really caught Ruth's attention since that is what she had come out wearing.

Whatever the case, he was glad to hear the *kinner* behaving for Mary as they came down for dinner.

Moses joined the *familye* for dinner at the dining room table. The vegetable stew had slowly replaced the smell of the burnt stew. Mary had always known how to throw something together in a hurry, even if it was relatively easy. It was a skill that Moses had never been able to develop, and he wasn't sure he was going to start now.

"How was your day with your *daed*?" Mary looked to the *kinner* after serving their dinners.

Moses remained quiet, eating his stew as if it had been a normal day of which he had little to say. The *kinner* hesitated as if they were not about to share what they had really been doing all day long.

"We weren't as good for him as we are for you, *Mamm*," Faith finally admitted. "But we wanted to play outside! And he wouldn't take us outside again after our naps."

"Do I take you outside after your nap if I'm working on dinner and the laundry?" Mary raised an eyebrow. "Even just to the porch? You all ought to know better than to make such a mess in the *haus*. I don't care what you wanted to do. If your *daed* said that you were not to go outside and that you needed to do something that wouldn't make a mess, that is what you should have done. He is your *daed*, not just some stranger that stays with us."

"*Jah, Mamm*."

"I'm sorry, *Daed*."

Ruth only nodded in addition to these statements, with her mouth full of food. At the very least, she was eating tonight, which was good. Moses didn't envy Mary's struggles to get Ruth to eat much during the day, and he wondered how she had the energy to make such a mess when she wasn't eating much at all during the day.

"Apologies accepted," Moses said softly. "It's been an interesting week for your *mamm* and me, and we appreciate that you're trying to be *gut*."

He didn't want to make it any harder for Mary in her day-to-day life, but he did appreciate that there were elements to childcare and housekeeping that he hadn't even thought of before. Before this week, he'd not realized that it was possible to burn a stew. He'd thought the water and stock that made up the majority of the dish kept that from happening.

Having been proven very wrong, he was not excited to learn what else he was wrong about.

Once dinner was done, he volunteered to do the dishes. Mary accepted gracefully and went off to read the *kinner* a Bible story. He might have been her favorite person to listen to when reading Bible stories, but he felt that she deserved time with the *kinner* today and he deserved some time not worrying about them being messy.

As he started on the dishes, Moses couldn't help but wonder what Mary had thought of Mr. Riverton. Surely he had been making problems for her just as he had for Moses. How had his *fraa* handled it, and did she understand why he didn't share everything with her when it happened?

CHAPTER 12

Mary put the *kinner* to bed that night, making sure they understood that just because Moses wasn't usually helping with the day-to-day process of taking care of them that didn't mean that they were allowed to cause such problems for him. He was their *daed* and as such his word was as powerful as Mary's as to what they could and could not do.

When she came out to the living room, she sat beside Moses and took his hands in hers.

"Now... where do we begin?" Moses said with a soft laugh. "It's only been two days, and I've already learned so much."

"Well... I met a rather interesting *Englisch* man who was dead set on making sure that you lost a lot of customers or a lot of money, perhaps both," Mary admitted. "Mr. Riverton is his name. Said the furniture you delivered to him was full of termites, but wouldn't provide any photos or proof of the termites. I guess you already know all of this, but I handled the situation."

Moses raised an eyebrow.

"How did you do that? I have been trying to *kumm* up with ways to get the money that he wants so that we can pay him off and be done with it all. He's costing me business, standing in front of the door all day calling me a cheat." He shook his head. "What did you do?"

"There is a certain subset of *Englischer* who will do whatever it takes to get ahead in life, often scamming businesses for refunds. I believe he was one of them, and I ended up talking to Jackson. While we were talking, he showed me some photos that Mr. Riverton had taken of the furniture."

From here, Mary described what she had done confronting Mr. Riverton, and how he had handled it. She wasn't entirely shocked that he had decided to run away from the problem, knowing that Mary wouldn't take his word for it and pay him as Moses had been about to.

"Wow," Moses said. "I'm very lucky to have

you as my *fraa*. I wouldn't have known that paying him out would bring more trouble to our shop."

"You don't know unless you've seen it before," Mary admitted. "I suspected we had someone like that from the way he was calling for our shop to be boycotted. But after all of this, I have a new-found appreciation for all that you do and all that you deal with to provide for us."

She squeezed his hand.

"I'm quite lucky that the *Englisch* neighbor was willing to help me out with all of this," she continued. "I don't know that I would have been able to find the proof I needed to get him to leave the shop on my own."

"Jackson is many things, and a *gut mann* has always been on that list," Moses said softly. "However, I am unbelievably sorry that I misunderstood what you do all day long. In this religion, motherhood and being a homemaker aren't viewed as being difficult since so many women are able to do it with a smile on their faces. I realize now that there's a lot more work that goes into it. Two days, and I was utterly unprepared for all of the chaos that *kinner* can create if you don't watch them carefully when they are full of energy."

"That's not the only reason I wanted to be a teacher again."

"That I understand as well now. When we started this, I didn't realize that you don't get to see other adults unless you arrange to take the *kinner* with you or receive an unexpected visitor. While I was home, no one came to see how I was doing until you arrived home from the shop, and I am so ready to see other adults. I actually almost feel *bad* that I need attention from someone else."

Mary laughed a little.

"Adult attention is always a good thing. It keeps us sane," she reasoned. "Other parents are always willing to help with that, even if it means that there are more *kinner* in the *haus* than normal for a little while. A walk in the snow helps, too, at this time of year."

"The only thing that I cannot understand now that we've done this little experiment," Moses confided, "is why on earth you'd wish to interact with more *kinner* each day. There's already enough chaos here at home. What is the appeal of teaching if you want to have more adult interaction instead of seeking out more time to be with *kinner*, even if they are not our own?"

"You really wish to know?"

Out of all the reasons she had agreed to do

this little swap, she had never realized that Moses hadn't quite realized that teaching wasn't standing in front of and giving attention to a classroom full of students. In its most basic definition, he was right about what the job entailed, but there was so much more to it. She wondered if he had ever really had his heart in it, or if he had always thought that he was doing it to pass time and wasn't in it for the *kinner*.

"I do." Moses let out a soft sigh. "When I taught here in Dalton, I did it because I needed a job and didn't quite have the funds to justify a carpentry shop. Subbing in the *Englisch* school was more for a change of pace, a chance to see if I had been as *gut* a teacher as people told me I had been. I must have been, because I was getting requests for months to sub again, though I didn't want to. For you to willingly look for employment as a teacher, I just... I want to understand what's driving you to make that choice. It clearly isn't because you want more time with the *kinner* since you get that every day they're home while I'm at the shop."

She nodded.

"Being in a classroom full of *kinner* is different than trying to parent," she started. "There's a fundamental difference in the way they'll treat a teacher versus a parent. A teacher can tell a student's parent that they're being difficult in class, and here in the community, they'll usually rectify the problem. In an *Englisch* school, the school board is more worried about test scores and making sure the parents can't cause more problems than the students do."

She looked to Moses to see if he was following, but she found his mouth open wide. Perhaps the fact that the parents in an *Englisch* school could be more trouble than the *kinner* was news to him, since he was only a sub and substitutes didn't usually see that kind of behavior.

"Wow."

"I know," Mary agreed. "But, here in Dalton, I enjoy being a teacher more than I ever did in an *Englisch* school, especially now that our *kinner* are going to be in school. Despite her tendency to make a huge mess when she gets curious, Ruth is a sweet young girl. I think the school system will do her some good since routine does her good. And... seeing me there might help her remember that there is always a chance someone could tell me what she does."

"Or that you'll see it yourself," Moses said with a laugh. "So, you're not hoping to join in the middle of the year, then?"

"*Ach, nee*, of course not."

"Then when, if you don't mind my asking? After all of this, I no longer think you were wrong to apply, but we needed to sit down and talk about it before you submitted that application. Edna came to me for advice on the best applicant for the job and, if it hadn't been for my frustrations with how you were handling the situation I think I would have told her much sooner that you'd be perfect for the job."

"I want to join next year when Ruth's old enough to start school, ideally," Mary admitted. "The timing was too perfect, and I wasn't thinking clearly when I submitted my application, thinking that you wouldn't know until it was too late to stop me from doing anything. You're the elder now, and that's a huge confidence for you. You need to know that I'm going to be there for you."

"And for our *kinner*. I'm the one the community is going to look to for advice in tough situations, and they're going to want me to deal with *Englischers* that don't quite understand what our community stands for. Everyone wanted me to deal with Mr. Riverton and make him go away, and I should have *kumm* to you for help before you went to the shop."

Mary squeezed his hands softly before pressing a kiss to his cheek.

"We all have our faults, and you have all your reasons for wanting to keep me from feeling more anxious than I already do with our *kinner*," she said. "But I do believe we have accomplished what we set out to do with swapping jobs for a week."

Moses nodded, putting his arms around her instead of holding her hands in his.

"And any hurt feelings mended," he said quietly. "You deserve the chance to interact with other adults, and I'm sorry that you felt that you had to sneak behind my back to get something like that."

"It's not your fault that you didn't understand, and I appreciate that you took the time to learn why I wanted to apply," she said. "Now... I think we've both had an exhausting day. I think it's about time we got to bed and enjoyed a good sleep. For one, I'm exhausted just from doing all the baby rattles. My fingers hurt."

"You actually did some carpentry?" Moses looked at her, shocked. "I didn't expect you to do any this week."

"I can do baby rattles, though you might have to refine some. And I made a few that weren't just circular on top," she admitted. "Some *familyes* are really into specific themes for boys and girls, and so I made crown-shaped rattles for the two *familyes* who specified they were having *dochders*, and an elephant rattle for the one having a *sohn* since Elijah liked his so much."

Moses smiled.

"I think they're going to love those," he said softly. "But for now, you're right. We ought to be going to bed."

With that, they both stood up from the couch. As they walked into the bedroom, Moses trailed his hand down her arm to hold her hand.

"For now, I plan on having a great Christmas with a *familye* I'm grateful for before you ask what my plans are between now and when Ruth enters school," Mary said, noticing that he looked a little torn. "But we can discuss details further when we aren't tired."

Moses nodded.

"I'm just glad to know that you appreciate us," he said softly as they walked to the bed. "You and the *kinner* are my everything, Mary. This community has always been there for me, but you're my *fraa*, my *familye*. You are the most important person in my life."

Mary blushed, hiding in his chest.

They shared a soft kiss before Mary pulled away to get into the bed. As she pulled the blankets up around her shoulders, Moses left to make sure the fire in the living room was safely extinguished before they went to bed. The last thing they needed tonight was a reason to worry about the *haus* or the *kinner* being hurt.

He returned shortly thereafter. It didn't take Mary long to fall asleep, dreaming of a happy life with her husband and her *kinner* for years to come.

EPILOGUE

A few years passed pleasantly, and soon enough another Christmas came around. Faith and Elijah were just about to leave the Amish schooling system, and Ruth had a couple more years left. Mary sat in the living room, grading papers, as she listened to her *kinner* share details about their lives while they hung pine boughs with Moses.

"I'm excited to see what the new year holds," Faith admitted quickly. "What kinds of jobs can I do here in Dalton once I'm done with school? When can I go on my *rumspringa*? Can I stay with Uncle George and his *familye* for some of it to see what that city is like?"

Mary laughed.

"You still have a couple of years before your *rumspringa* comes along, Faith," she said without looking up from one of the assignments. "However, once we get closer to the time for that, I'm sure we could call both George and Brian and see if either would be interested in hosting you for a little while. You'd have to take the train, of course, or find a ride out there."

"I think I'd like to stay closer to home when my *rumspringa* comes," Elijah piped up. "A couple of my friends and I are thinking about looking into renting an apartment together here in town and coming home every weekend so we can get a taste of both lives. That's the best way to find out, isn't it?"

He looked to her.

"There's always going to be a shock," she warned, "but just as I told Faith, you've still got a couple of years before you have to worry. Worry about being with your friends for now. About making memories you'll look back on fondly one day."

"I agree with your *mamm* on that one," Moses piped up. "Don't remind me that I've got *kinner* almost old enough for their *rumspringas*. Give me at least one more Christmas where I can pretend like I don't have to worry about your plans, please."

This caused all of them to start laughing.

"Well, I'm excited to see what Spring holds," Ruth declared. "My friends and I want to make quilts for *bopplin* due in Spring, but I'm not sure what kind of quilt to make to start with. There are so many *gut* quilt designs."

"That there are," Mary said. "Well, for now, I suggest you all focus on Christmas. It's a *Wunderbar* season of the year, and it only lasts a few weeks."

"She's right, you know," Moses continued. "It's freshly snowed, and I think you've all got friends that are waiting to exchange gifts with you. When are you supposed to do that again?"

He looked over at Mary, who had momentarily looked up at the clock.

All three of their *kinner* gasped and started to hurry through the *haus*. Faith grabbed the small gifts she had made, while Elijah grabbed the gifts that his *daed* had helped him make for his friends. Ruth had decided to make aprons for her friends, and her arms were the fullest as she pulled her cloak over her shoulders.

"We'll be home before dinner," Elijah said. "We promise. Right, Faith, Ruth?"

"We promise!" the two girls answered in unison as they pulled their boots on. Mary only smiled. She didn't care when they came home so long as they arrived home safely before bedtime. However, she wasn't going to tell them that. Having them home for dinner sounded like a beautiful idea, and she knew that if she gave them permission, they'd stay out all night to play in the snow with their friends.

"That's *gut* to hear," Mary said.

With that, their *kinner* walked out the door. The door's soft slam echoed momentarily through the *haus* as Mary set her papers down.

"As much as I love them, I thought they were never leaving," Moses teased. "Would you like a cup of *kaffe*? A chance to rest your eyes, perhaps? You've been grading papers for a long while."

"I'd love a cup of *kaffe*, actually," Mary said softly. "I've been falling a little bit behind and needed to get all of this done so that I could give it all to Edna. She wants to get it returned when the *kinner* go back to school in the new year."

"Ah. That would explain the massive stack of papers to grade."

Mary nodded as she stretched her fingers, and then her neck. It was a bit of a struggle, grading papers all day long, but now that her *kinner* were old enough that they could be self-sufficient, it wasn't as bad as when they were younger.

Moses poured her a cup of *kaffe* and they sat at the dining room table. Through the window, they could see the freshly fallen snow with three sets of footprints through it – one for each of their *kinner* who had left to exchange gifts with their friends.

Mary took her husband's hand softly.

"I feel at peace with my life this way," she said. "Fulfilled, perhaps, is the better word. I have a loving *familye*, and that's really all I ever wanted. A *familye* I could call my own, and who wouldn't write me off because they'd gotten married and had their own lives too."

Moses squeezed her hand softly as he swallowed his *kaffe*.

"I'm glad to hear it because I cannot imagine life any other way," he said. "Marrying you was the best thing I've ever done, Mary, and I would be remiss if I did not share that with you. Fulfilled is a very good word for how it feels. If I'm not mistaken, we share that feeling."

He smiled at her before putting his cup down and taking her cheek in his hand. She pressed her cheek into his hand in response.

"I could not imagine my life any differently now that I'm here with you," she admitted. "And I'm glad to know that you feel the same way."

Click here to get notification when the next book is available, and to hear about other good things I give my readers (or copy and paste this link into your browser: *bit.ly/Grace-FreeBook*). **You will also receive a free copy of *Rumspringa's Promise, Secret Love* and *River Blessings*, exclusive spinoffs from the *Seasons of Love, Amish Hearts* and the *Amish Sisters series*** for members of my Readers' Group. These stories are NOT available anywhere else.

FREE DOWNLOAD

EXCLUSIVE and FREE for subscribers of my Readers' Group

CLICK HERE!

amazon kindle

(or copy and paste this link into your browser: *bit. ly/Grace-FreeBook*)

NOTE FROM THE AUTHOR

Thank you for taking a chance on *Christmas Awakening,* Book 5 of the *Amish Christmas Blessings* series.

Did you enjoy the book? I hope so, and I would really appreciate it if you would help others enjoy this book, and help spread the word.

Please consider leaving a review today telling other readers why you liked this book, wherever you purchased this book, or on Goodreads. **It doesn't need to be long,** just a few sentences can make a huge difference. **Your reviews go a long way in helping others discover what I am writing,** and decide if a book is for them.

I appreciate anything you can do to help, and if you do write a review, wherever it is, please send an email at grace@gracelewisauthor.com, so I could thank you personally.

Here are some places where you can leave a review:

- Amazon.com;
- Goodreads.

Thank you for reading, and have a lovely day,

Grace Lewis

PS: I love hearing from my readers. Feel free to email me directly at grace@gracelewisauthor.com (or to connect with me on Facebook here https://www.facebook.com/GraceLewisAuthor). I read and respond to every message.

EXCLUSIVE CHRISTMAS BOXSET: 15 TALES OF LOVE, FAMILY AND CHRISTMAS CELEBRATION

Dear Readers,

Thank you for immersing yourselves in the heartwarming world of our *Amish Christmas Blessings* series. As the festive season wraps you in its warm embrace, we're thrilled to bring you an exclusive opportunity to dive even deeper into the enchanting tales of love, faith, and family.

For a limited time this Christmas, we are delighted to offer a special boxset that contains not only the first 15 books of our beloved series but also includes the 4 previous books of *Amish Christmas Blessings* series. It's a treasure trove of stories that will fill your holidays with the spirit of Amish romance and the magic of Christmas.

>> **Copy and paste this link: amazon.com/dp/B0CKQBF7R4** into your browser to get this special 15 books Boxset including the previous books of the *Amish Christmas Blessings* series.

But that's not all! The journey doesn't end here. We're excited to announce that the final story in this series is on its way, and it promises to be as captivating and heartwarming as ever. As a token of our appreciation for your continued support, you will find an excerpt from this upcoming book hereafter.

Don't miss this chance to own this special collection. It's the perfect way to cozy up and enjoy the holiday season, wrapped in the tender and inspiring tales of our Amish community.

>> **Copy and paste this link: amazon.com/dp/B0CKQBF7R4** into your browser to get this special 15 books Boxset including the previous books of the *Amish Christmas Blessings* series.

Warm wishes and happy reading,

Grace Lewis

OTHER BOOKS BY GRACE LEWIS

Click here to browse all Grace Lewis's Books (or copy and paste this link into your browser: *bit.ly/ gracelewisauthor*).

AGAINST ALL HOPE – AMISH CHRISTMAS BLESSINGS SERIES, BOOK 6 (EXCERPT)

Against all Hope Summary

This Christmas, the Lapp family must find a way to triumph over adversity and save their community.

In the gripping finale of our cherished series, a crisis looms over the Amish community during the most festive time of the year. Thanksgiving brings a chilling revelation: the crops have failed, threatening a winter of scarcity.

Mary, ever the pillar of strength, takes a bold step outside her comfort zone, leaving her Amish teaching post to work in an Englischer school. Simultaneously, Moses, driven by a deep love for his community, embarks on an ambitious expansion of his wood store to meet the demands of the Christmas season. Their decisions, made in desperation to save their community, strain not only their marriage but also their beliefs.

As tensions rise, an unexpected arrival adds fuel to the fire. Mary's friend Millie, burdened with personal struggles and accompanied by her two children, seeks refuge with the Lapps. Her presence tests the already fragile threads of friendship and family.

In a community where unity is paramount, will these challenges fracture the bonds that hold them together, or will the spirit of Christmas inspire a miracle? With time running out and the cold intensifying, a daring proposal for a fundraiser emerges. Can Mary, Moses, and Millie overcome their differences and rally the community for a common cause?

Prepare for a journey of faith, resilience, and the power of community in the face of adversity. *Against All Hope* invites you to experience the true spirit of Christmas in a story where love, sacrifice, and hope converge. Will this Christmas bring the miracle they need? Don't miss the heartwarming conclusion to this beloved series.

>> **copy and paste this link into your**

CHAPTER ONE

Moses sat at the table in the boarding *haus*, looking around. Thanksgiving and Christmas had become his favorite times of the year. They were the two celebrations of the year when the community gathered for a large celebration somewhere in the community. For Thanksgiving, they gathered here. Over Christmas, they gathered for a large Christmas pageant in someone's barn, as it was the equivalent of their service that week.

He noticed that there was one person he had not seen at the dinner yet: Amos Lantz.

Amos was one of the elders in the community who was a particularly moody man. Lately, it felt as though he was in a dark mood, which Moses had yet to find the reason for. He'd thought it was just because it had been a particularly harsh winter. The snow had already started to fall hard and thick, although it was only November.

Dalton had seen snow like this before, but it never made anyone in the community tense. He knew there was some talk of crops failing, but every year they had one or two plants that didn't want to flower for whatever reason. They'd maneuvered through it fine before. He was sure the community would survive whatever was coming its way this year, too.

He walked towards Addie Miller, standing by the main buffet line with a pleasant smile on her face. The Thanksgiving feast was one of her points of pride, being the owner of the lodging *haus* they used for it every year.

"*Hallo*, Moses," Addie said. "Want more food? There's plenty to go around. I'll probably be sending people home with some food, too. Don't want it to go to waste."

"Not yet, but *danke* for the offer," Moses replied. "I'm more curious about something else. Have you seen Amos today?"

He pursed his lips as he waited for Addie to answer. She had grabbed a sweet roll as he spoke, and her mouth was currently full. She swallowed and then hesitated for a moment.

"If I'm honest, you're the only elder I've seen here tonight," she said. "Haven't seen any of them today. It's odd. Perhaps you know what they're all in a fuss about?"

"I wouldn't know, but I have a couple of ideas. *Danke,* Addie. That's more of an answer than anyone else would have given me, I believe."

With that, he went to sit down with his *fraa*.

"What was that all about, Moses?" Mary looked over at him.

Their *kinner* were currently enjoying story-telling, the ambiance set before the fire blazing in the fireplace. Other *kinner* had gathered to join in or tell their own stories when it was their turn. It gave all the parents a break. In fact, this entire gathering was partially geared towards giving the parents the chance to enjoy each other's company and let the small ones enjoy a good meal without having to worry about anything else.

"I was just curious about where Amos and the rest of the elders seem to have gotten to," he admitted. "I guess they should join the festivities later. Hopefully, they show up soon. It does not look good to have only one elder in the room with such a large crowd."

Mary nodded slowly. That much they could agree on.

Slowly, the rest of the elders started to arrive. Moses didn't care that they were about half an hour later than he was, or that the feast had started without them. They arrived. However, Amos remained absent from the room.

Moses did his best not to focus on the absence. This was Thanksgiving. It wasn't the night to focus on any of the issues within the community. The past year had been decent to them, but the ruckus with Mr. Riverton had caused some business issues. Moses wasn't sure his business would fully recover until next year, but he was hopeful that he might be wrong.

As the fire continued to blaze, Moses got up and started talking to others in the community. The rest of the *kinner* welcomed Mary onto the floor with them. She had been teaching for a while, and they all loved having her in the classroom.

He started with Edna.

"Oh, a pleasure to see you, Moses," Edna said. "Mary and the *kinner* look just perfect, don't you think?"

"*Jah.* She's a blessing in the classroom, I bet." Moses offered her a small smile.

"She is. I'm glad that she was interested in the job."

"How have you been?"

"*Gut, gut.* It's been busy in the classroom, but when isn't it busy?" Edna laughed.

He continued around the room and made sure to talk to some of the elderly residents of the community who had made it out tonight. The rest would end up getting food delivered to them by relatives or friends who were here.

When he made it back to those in front of the fire, his job was done. He got himself another sweet roll before taking his seat. As the food eventually dwindled and people started leaving with leftovers, Moses helped Mary bundle their *kinner* up to get back on the road.

Faith, Ruth, and Elijah were not happy to be leaving, but they all understood that the night was coming to an end.

That was until Amos entered the room.

"Addie, would you mind taking the *kinner* into another room for a little while, or showing us to a room where we can talk?" Amos looked to Addie. "I don't think this is something that they need to hear."

"*Mamm*, what does he mean?"

"It's all right, Ruth. Go with Addie."

"Here. You three follow me," Addie said, pointing to Mary, Moses, and Amos. "You can use the kitchen. I'll take the *kinner* to the parlor for now. I'm sure there's plenty of snow to see out the window after being here as long as we have." She gave everyone a soft smile.

Moses nodded. With that, Mary and Amos

followed him into the kitchen. Meanwhile, Addie took the *kinner* into the parlor. The windows were on the wall furthest from the kitchen, which would make this easier to discuss.

"We missed you at dinner, Amos," Mary said softly. "Why is it that you arrived after everyone has left?"

"The community will not survive the winter," Amos declared, "unless we are able to come up with the money to buy our food throughout the winter. Too many crops have failed this year."

Moses's stomach dropped. *Too many* crops failed? That hadn't happened in many years, and there were safeguards in place to make sure that this could be taken care of before Thanksgiving. Why had he only just heard of it now?

"*Too many* of them?" Moses furrowed his eyebrows, managing to hide the fact that his stomach was starting to do flips. "How could you hide this from us, Amos?"

"I was hoping that we would be able to find a solution before it became this dire," Amos admitted. "However, everything we came up with failed. It was me who convinced the rest of the elders to hide this from you. My hope was that we would not have to share the dire situation until we'd found a way to soften the blow.

Clearly... I was unable to prevent that from happening."

Moses pursed his lips. He had been counting on Amos and the other elders to make sure that the community would be able to get through the winter. After Mr. Riverton disrupted his business last year, his business had been struggling. He couldn't help the community if he couldn't take care of his own *familye*.

"What does this mean for the community?" Mary spoke quietly as if her mind was still attempting to process what they had heard.

Moses wouldn't have blamed her for excusing herself from the conversation at this point. However, her *Englischer* childhood might offer a unique solution here.

"It means I am sure that we will not make it through the whole winter. This will be the toughest winter we've faced in many years. I am sorry that it has come to this, of course, but what else can we do? There is nothing more to try. The ground is already covered in snow, and we do not have the means to start crops now. Even if we could start crops now, they wouldn't be ready in time for us to harvest them before feeling the effects of this failure. Winter is at our doors, there is not much left to harvest by then except root vegetables."

Moses rubbed his temples.

"We'll find a way to make sure the community comes through the winter without feeling the hardship too much," he said softly. "But next time, you need to speak up while there is still time to fix it before the need gets dire. I'm not sure what we'll be able to do now."

Amos nodded slowly and then walked out of the room.

Moses turned to Mary.

"Have you ever had to deal with something like this before, Moses?" Mary's voice quivered.

He shook his head.

"Joseph might have as an elder, but if he had, we never felt the issue as seriously as we will this year," Moses replied. "I'm not sure what we can do. If most of the crops have failed, then we need to find a solution sooner rather than later. And it won't be easy to buy food for the entire community. The *Englischers* are not always as kind to us as you might imagine, considering the way we treat them."

"I've noticed," Mary commented. "But for now, I say we at least get our *kinner* to bed before we discuss this any further. You're a community elder now, and this is going to be your life. Let me help you find a way to deal with the problem. Because the others have stalled so long, you now need the help."

He nodded. That much, she had a point on. Anything he could think of now would have been applicable at the end of the harvest season, not this close to the winter season.

"Will you go collect them from Addie? I need a moment alone to gather my thoughts and contain the anger. I cannot believe they thought that it would be all right to hide this issue from me when I could have helped."

Mary nodded and walked out of the kitchen.

Now alone, Moses took in a deep breath. In the few years he had been an elder, nothing of this magnitude had come up. He supposed it was only a matter of time before a major trial had come up, but to hear that most of the crops had failed was not what he had thought his first major crisis would be.

Mary applying to work alongside Edna and Mr. Riverton's wish to ruin his business all seemed so small compared to the imminent threat of failed crops and the prospect of the community going without food.

Admitting defeat only for today, he took one

last deep breath, inhaling and then exhaling. He let go as much of the anger as he could before joining his *familye* and Addie in the parlor.

"Is everything all right, Moses?" Addie raised an eyebrow.

Moses gave her a curt nod.

"It's fine." He resisted the urge to add the words 'for now.'

With that, he helped Mary corral the *kinner* into their buggy and they made their way home. Once they were home, it didn't take long for everyone to admit they were exhausted. Thanksgiving was one of the few days of the year on which the *kinner* didn't have to go to bed at a set time. But they were usually ready for bed by the time the dinner was over if they had it with the entire community.

Mary didn't even have to do much. She simply sent them up to their rooms, calling a good night after each of them.

"Now… I think we could do with some sleep, too," Mary admitted. "We've been working all day long to make sure that the dinner was successful, and now we have something else to worry about. Perhaps we'll think of something in the morning if we're able to sleep on it."

Moses nodded.

"You always have the most logical response in the moment," he said. "I appreciate it."

>> copy and paste this link into your browser: *bit.ly/Grace-FreeBook* to be notified when the book is available.

THE SEASONS OF LOVE SERIES

The Seasons of Love series follows the journey of seven siblings in an Amish community as they navigate their desires and dreams in life, which lead them to complicated relationships with each other and potential suitors. The series shows the unbreakable bond between the Mast siblings as they face the ups and downs of their romantic lives.

Each book is a stand-alone read, but to make the most of the series you should consider reading them in order.

>> **Copy and paste this link: amazon.com/dp/B0BZ5BDK5Q into your browser to read it now.**

What readers are saying about the Seasons of Love series:

Book 1: Spring of Virtue

⭐⭐⭐⭐⭐ Grace Lewis did a wonderful job of writing this book. The characters had interesting personalities, the story line was different, and the outcome was endearing. I definitely recommend this book.

⭐⭐⭐⭐⭐ I loved the entire book. I didn't want to put it down. The characters came to life as I read the story.

Book 2: Summer of Longing

⭐⭐⭐⭐⭐ I am really enjoying this series. Each story is very well written and each of them are different. I look forward to reading all of them.

⭐⭐⭐⭐⭐ **An Endearing Story, for sure!** I loved the main characters from the very beginning. I loved the way the story unfolded right before your eyes. Definitely a book to be recommended. The author wrote a truly lovely and welcoming story. Thank you.

Book 3: Indian Summer Turmoil

⭐⭐⭐⭐⭐ Indian Summer Turmoil is such a

delightful read. I love the characters and their real dilemmas. Trying to live out your life and make others happy is a burden God doesn't mean for us to carry. The Twists and turns are real and true love wins. Which makes a great read!

Book 4: Harvesting Hope

What a delicious read this was! I love the sweetness and the real emotional conflict of parents and daughter. You don't want to miss this one, for sure.

Book 5: Winter's Whisper

The series is fantastic! Every book turned out to be beautiful and fascinating. I truly went from one book to the next with passion to find out more.

Wonderful! This book was another can't put down until reading every word. I was so happy when Joanne decided to not marry the old man her Father's age. Sometimes patience is the name of the game. Year's ago, I had to learn to be patient, never thinking it would be that many year's.

Book 6: Blossoming into Family

Great series! I thoroughly enjoyed

every single book in this series! Each story was different, with a great lesson as well. Sometimes I do not like series books, but this one I thoroughly enjoyed.

☆☆☆☆☆ A very sweet short story of how great it is to feel like you are accepted, cared for and loved. How great it is to have a close family.

>> Copy and paste this link: amazon.com/dp/B0BZ5BDK5Q into your browser to read it now.

This book is a work of fiction. Names, characters and places are either products of the author's imagination or used fictitiously. Any resemblance to actual persons, living or dead, events, locales or Amish communities is entirely coincidental. The author has taken liberties with locales, including the creation of fictional towns and places, as a mean of creating the necessary circumstances for the story. This books is intended for fictional purposes only, it is not a handbook on the Amish.

www.ingramcontent.com/pod-product-compliance
Lightning Source LLC
LaVergne TN
LVHW040022120325
805731LV00033B/938